CITYMUSE

Nelson Lowhim

Also By Nelson Lowhim

When Gods Fail

Tree of Freedom

The Struggle Trilogy

When Gods Fail II

Rebel

Alternative Book Press
2 Timber Lane
Suite 301
Marlboro, NJ 07746
www.alternativebookpress.com

2013 Paperback Edition
Copyright 2013 © Nelson Lowhim
Cover Illustration by Nelson Lowhim
Book Design by Nelson Lowhim
Published in the United States of America by Alternative Book Press

Originally published in electronic form in the United States by Alternative
Book Press.
Library of Congress Cataloging-in-Publication Data

Nelson, Lowhim, [date]
CityMuse/ by Nelson, Lowhim.—1st ed.
p. cm.
1. City and Town Life (Fiction). I Title.
PN370-380.L69C589   2013
813'.6—dc23
2013912327

ISBN 978-1-940122-05-2
Printed in the United States of America
10 9 8 7 6 5 4 3 2 1

Dedicated to all the veterans, and damned souls trying to make sense of it all.

Table of Contents:

J enny was gorgeous.

I first met her in a coffee shop in the village. I loved her thighs glistening beneath her summer shorts and small-melon breasts bulging out from her shirt. Her face was smooth with a thick lower lip and up-turned prep school nose.

We met up a few days later in the village. In a café that was blasting cold air, stifling all the usual smells that summer charmed from living beings. I talked to her about what she did: worked as a consultant in some financial firm. She didn't seem to mind it; in fact thought it was dandy, earning beaucoup money and what not. She was from Long Island, but spent most of her youth here in the City. Then went to Columbia. She was dressed in a summer dress and cleavage that was just enough to tantalize. The dress was short and her legs shone like they had the day before.

"Travel much?"

"Oh, here and there," she said and twirled her hair; I was getting to her.

"Where?"

"Paris, London..."

I stopped listening when she named cities instead of countries. The few times she mentioned a country, I inquired further only to get the name of some resort. Cancun isn't Mexico. She twirled her hair some more, bit her lip, and all was forgiven.

"You travel?"

"A lot. My job requires it."

"Oh and what do you work as?"

Ah the question I could not answer. I smiled at her and sipped my coffee.

"It's a consultant business. But mainly I do it for the government." I looked her over quickly then wondered if I should have added any sugar or cream to my coffee. It was barely drinkable, and here we were in a fancy New York City café. The girl behind the counter, with her excessive tattoos and piercings, looked like something the village had been spewing out for decades.

"Like what exactly?"

"Security type stuff." I sipped the coffee again, trying to get as little into my mouth as possible. There was a background flavor of burned beans, and I couldn't get around this taste.

She looked me over. "Coffee not good?"

"It's fine. Nothing like Paris though, right?"

"Oh, it's amazing in Paris."

"Well, I can't exactly talk about what I do. Not that I won't. It's just that it's sensitive and that once I've gotten to know you I can trust you with some of the information."

She looked at me incredulously, waiting for me to break out into a smile. I could tell.

"This isn't a joke is it?"

"No. I know it sounds ridiculous, and if you don't believe me, or think this is some trick then let me know. Because it won't work out then."

She moved uncomfortably in her seat then looked at me. Eye contact suddenly as fierce as a warrior tribesman's. I stayed calm and looked into her blue eyes. I noticed that they were especially reflective, shiny orbs.

"Okay," she murmured not acting quite certain with the whole situation.

"Thank you. If it helps I can't tell too many people about what I do. Not even my family."

That seemed to soften the blow for her, and we dived into the issue of my family: the distance, the happiness in leaving the small town for something so grand and shiny like the City.

I moved us out to Washington Square. She carelessly bumped her hand into mine. I grasped her finger, felt her cede way, and moved up to hold her hand. I looked at her and forced myself not to smile. She looked down again. Was she shy or cynical? I couldn't quite tell.

At the square we watched performers, mostly black, dance in somersaults for the mostly light-skinned loungers. Some were entertaining, pulling in the crowd then going for broke with scary flips. I tossed some money into their hats.

"So how did you get into your line of work?"

I paused, looking off to the distance. She was examining me again. Using those cynical City eyes to see if there was so much as a hint that I was making all this up. If I stumbled for a second she would be gone.

A deer in the woods.

My finger on the trigger.

This flesh was mine.

"I was in the military before. In special operations." I paused, still talking in drips. The word I used was a generic term if ever I heard one, but it was used because getting any more specific would lead to confusion. After all, she was a civilian. In this day and age in America, that meant that she didn't know fuck-all about the military.

"Wow, that is something."

"Do you know anything about it? About special operations?" If she did know I was still good. If she didn't I would just stay away from specifics.

"No, I think I've heard of it, though." She smiled and looked away before moving closer to me.

My heart jumped, and I stopped my mind from racing about and imagining her without her clothes on. She was gorgeous when she smiled. Should have done it more often. Perhaps it attracted too many men.

I took her all the way up to MOMA and asked her if she wanted to see some of Picasso's paintings.

We walked in and I explained a few paintings. Every time I told her to look at the facture of a painting she leaned in and I glanced at her thighs and ass as it pushed out from the dress. The beast within reared its head. I weighed my options. It was always good to leave while the going was good and try to set something up for later. Never overplay your hand. Yet I felt that it was all too good to cut off at that point. I could just push my luck and see how far she would let me go. After all, this city was full of women like her. It wouldn't be hard to find another.

But time. Oh time.

After we finished with the museum, we walked out and battled the crowds by going towards the village again.

"You know what I could go for?"

"What?" she asked.

"A really good cup of coffee."

"I know just the place."

"Here?"

"My place." She looked me over. "You don't mind do you?"

"No."

Her place was perfect. All right, I lie, it was a cute apartment, but it was perfectly situated. The floor plan isn't what enticed me. It was that feeling of walking in and smelling a clean, perfume encrusted apartment of a woman I didn't truly know. That sense of being allowed into a sensitive part of her life was strong, and I stopped my hands from grabbing her around the waist. I didn't make a move. Instead I waited for my coffee to come out of her expensive looking espresso machine, and sat down with her. Better to be cool and calm in situations like these.

"So Mr. Special Operations, you like?"

She, so shy only a few hours ago, was now bold. A predator. I didn't mind. Cool calm, like the wave. Crash when you want, just crest for now. I was looking at her paintings on the wall. She had good taste. All were original works with a contrast of colors that spoke to my inner madman.

"I love these. Where did you get them?"

"Art fairs around the world. Pretty cheap, actually."

"You got them all?"

"Of course. You don't think I have an artistic eye, Mr. Facture?" she spoke and flashed me a half smile.

I sipped the rest of my coffee. Her coffee was chocolaty with hints of a spice I couldn't put my finger on.

"I never said that." I glanced at her eyes to see how long she would hold the stare. She didn't look away. She was on the offensive. I liked this Jenny better. I reached over and brushed the hair from her cheek, placing it behind her ear. She maintained eye contact, though I could tell she held her breath. "It's just indicative of amazing taste."

"I know what I like when I see it," she said, still holding eye contact.

I sipped the last of the coffee and placed it down. My heart was slowly picking up its rate as I stepped to her and ran my finger down her cheek.

"Is that a fact?"

"Yes," she whispered.

"And do you like what you see now?"

"Very much."

Those words, that gate opening, flushed my brain. I used every ounce of self-restraint not to rip her clothes off.

Kiss.

Kiss.

Kiss.

Touch.

Kiss.

Kiss.

Kiss.

Stroke.

Kiss.

Kiss.

Kiss.

Touch.

Stroke.

As she moaned I reached down. She didn't stop me.

We fucked in her living room, her dress still on, her perfect ass on her dining table. I didn't last long, I'll admit. I fucked only to get rid of a tick in my mind. Then came with the force of a shotgun.

I didn't leave her apartment for two days. Neither did she. We fucked and only attended to the most basic of other needs in our life when we absolutely had to. Let me say one thing: she was amazing in bed. Not just because of her beauty and finely sculpted curves, which alone were enough to drive a man out of his mind, but because of the imagination and range of love or lust that she brought to the bedroom, hallway, walls, kitchens, floors. She was submissive, dominant and wanting. She told me she was certain that on our last session—when she had been cooking us a snack, and I accosted her in the kitchen—that she had been fucked like her mother did when she was conceived.

Yes, I liked her.

The next day I rushed out of her apartment after a shower. My wife had been calling me, and I had to go and see her, otherwise I would have to face her wrath. Not really any violence, but rather her quiet cold look, which, believe it or not, could strike my heart down. After all, I loved her dearly.

"Where were you?" the wife asked, scanning my face for some truth.

"No where honey, you know I have to get training done for the next job."

She took in a deep breath, hands crossed across her shoulders, staring at my eyes, like she always did when she felt a lie had been over the line.

I stepped forward to give her a hug, and she turned her head away. I hugged her anyways. What else could I say? I would die for any contact with her. Her coldness might not have been from me being away, but rather the fact that I was going on another contracting trip over to the Middle East. She hated that. Hated that I was going to face danger. I had told her about my past, spec ops and all those dirty little things, and she, like many other women, had been impressed by what she saw, but for her to remain impressed it had to—all that danger and killing and you know what—stay in the past. These contracting trips, no matter how little I told her to alleviate the pain, were always a stress on her. It was as if she somehow knew that I was in danger, and that I was lying to her about doing safe work in the Jordanian, or X country's, embassy. She knew me well. And why not? Hadn't we known each other for five years now?

"When are you leaving?"

"A few days now, so the training is going to pick up."

"And you can't tell me where you're going?" She pursed her beautiful red lips. I couldn't help but smile, she was sexy when her fury flew.

"You know I can't." I rubbed the backside of her arm. She looked off. Did she know about Jenny? No way, I was an expert and would know when I had been trailed and no silly private detective had been any where near me, but I could feel a distance grow between us. This part I could not live with. "It's going to be in Jordan, okay?"

She took in another deep breath. "You know I don't like that. You going to these places. I thought you were done."

"It's money we need baby." I forced a smile. This close to her, I could smell her tongue, it was as if she hadn't brushed her teeth all day. I thought of Jenny; her mouth always seemed like it was just brushed. I looked away for a second. This was bad practice, thinking of the other woman when I was with the wife.

"What are you thinking about?"

"Nothing, baby. Just the training, and the trip over there. I promise you once I'm done with this, I won't have to travel overseas again. All right?" It was more than a deflection of her suspicions; it was the truth. I had talked to the boss, and he said that the work back stateside was opening up. It would be different, but it would be in the same vein. "The trip should bring in almost a quarter million baby." I looked into her green eyes, which were getting wet.

"You know I don't care about that." She looked at me, her round face contorting with seriousness that seemed somewhat contrived.

She was, however, right. She didn't care, I knew that, always did, and never once did I doubt that. Reason I married her.

"I know honey, that's why I love you so much." I stroked her chin. Her face cracked out a smile, like sunrays on a rainy beach; it lit me up inside. I took her in my arms, kissed her a few times, and led her to our bedroom. I was exhausted, of course, from the weekend with Jenny, but I tried my hardest to keep a respectable grind going. In the end I had to fall back on my mouth. She came with the angst of a sunset on a cold winter's day.

She lay on top of me, her ear on my chest, looking at me like we were strangers. It shocked, me, made me wonder what was going on in her head. Our relationship required very little fine-tuning, we were usually on the same page, but when we were not, it hurt.

Bad.

Sunk my life into pits of despair.

I was glad to have at least pleased her. For all the exploration with the physically perfect Jenny, she could never match this feeling of pulling fibers within my heart, my brain, my balls, that my wife had.

I got up and walked up to our window. We lived in the Bronx, a small studio that did us well, but also kept the old lady pining for something better. "We'll be able to move after this trip baby." I turned to look at her body, intertwined in the sheets, her face peaking out. "I'll start looking as soon as I get back. All right?"

"What will you do for work?"

I hesitated for a second. I really didn't like telling her the specifics of what I did. "Same thing as now. But here in the states." I looked at the red brick buildings that populated our area here in the North Bronx. A subway slid before me. It was better at night, when I wrote like a madman, and the sparks off the third rail would bring me back with sudden explosions of the war—except these were silent.

Ahh, the City. *The* City. Always moving.

She moved behind me, her finger trailing on the small of my back. "You will be around here more?"

I thought for a second, better to not get her hopes up. "I will be here, but work will still be busy love." I could smell her skin: sweet, sour, sweaty, lovely.

She looked at me, sad, like I had yanked at her heart again. We were both very sensitive to the other. Like I said, finely tuned, only it was more like a shared heart, one we had to be careful of. I didn't like it; it was just the way things were.

"I will try to stay home more often," I whispered, knowing that I would try, but life would pull us apart once again. "I promise." I kissed her neck, on the vein she liked having touched.

We played a game of chess and I made dinner for her.

When we were done with that, each sitting in our separate parts of the room, reading out respective books, my phone vibrated.

Jenny, you'd better have more sense than to text me randomly, I thought. I tried to remember if I had told her my marital status yet. Possibly. I looked at the phone: Johnny. From Alaska.

What up, in town. Wanna grab some drinks?

Sure thing. Where you at? I texted back.

I looked at the old lady. It was getting near her bedtime. She had work at the school tomorrow early. She wouldn't be able to come out with us. That might have been for the better. I hadn't introduced her to Johnny just yet. And Johnny wasn't someone you introduced over drinks. Or all at once. It was better to introduce him in little bits, and with more stories up front.

"Who was that?"

"An old friend is in town. Might have to go out and meet him."

She didn't look up from her book. "It's late. Why don't you invite him over?"

Uh boy. Most likely that wouldn't be the wisest of choices. My contracting, done through the Department of Defense and the State Department, required a piss test. Johnny had a habit of making me unfit for those kinds of things. Especially if we were to hang out here. On the other hand, perhaps he would be tamer in front of the old lady.

Wash sq. You wanna get wasted?

That was not what I wanted.

Can you come over?

No reply. I looked at the old lady. Which would I prefer? Heading out, or enjoying a moment of the clash of classes within my room. My wife, ivy-educated, taught at Medical School in the City. She would not be one for the lower echelons of whitedom that Johnny hailed from. My phone started to ring.

"What's up Johnny? Been awhile, eh?" It had been a while. I hadn't seen him in a few years. And before that it was only a few sparse meets here and there. Always memorable, though, and always good to know there are people like him in the world. We had got to know each other when I was working up in Alaska, before my time in the military. Fellow slave laborer. He was a schemer. Said that we could corner the local weed market, no problem. So we got some muscle, and started to sell. Good thing about Alaska is that most everyone buys weed. Need it.

"Matt, you sonofabitch. What the hell have you been up to?"

"Nothing, what are you doing here?"

"You know, tying up some ends."

I paused. I thought I knew what that meant. Or at least what it could only have meant given his line of work. A small business owner, that's what he called himself. After a warrant had been issued for his arrest back in Alaska, he high-tailed it, barely missing the cops. Luckily it had been his face on all the posters. His little cabin they raided. No one suspected me. So I threw him in a hollowed out rear seat, and drove back to the continental States. Did I mention my smile was a million dollars? Got right through the checkpoint, and customs. We more or less parted ways after that; he further into the drug world, with assorted attempts at legal labor or education here and there, while I cleansed myself in the fires of the military. Army. Then spec ops. Funny how helpful having been a dealer was in that line of work.

"Well..." Was I really going to ask him to come over? I had more or less obeyed the law since I came over from the military, and since I met the wife I had been even better. Perhaps we could meet and let him stay for only a few drinks. "I'm up here in the Bronx. Come on over, you can meet the wife." She perked up when I said that, smiled at me. That would help things between us. Not a whipped man, but if it will make my life easier between me and the missus, I'll do it.

"Why the fuck not?"

"Good, you near the D-train?"

"Yep, that's the orange one, right?"

"Right. Take it to the northern end. I'll meet you there."

I read another chapter of *For Whom The Bells Tolls* before walking outside. It was a great book, real good refresher on the details of unconventional warfare.

I took in some air. It was another warm, humid night, the crickets chirped near the Williamsbridge oval. I heard a few kids ignoring the "closed at night" sign and skateboard off the ledges near the top of the park. Beautiful neighborhood we lived in. Well, for this part of the Bronx. A few muggings here and there, but nothing like it was in the 80s, or how it was purported to be in the South Bronx. A large man, hulking, bent at the back like he was lifting weights for too much of his life, in a hoodie walked towards me. I sidestepped the garbage and nodded at him. I had always wondered how easy it would be to mug someone. Just point a gun. Then what would they do? As long as you made sure to take their cell phone you would be able to get away. Wintertime, with more clothes would probably be better.

At the 205th stop I waited for Johnny. His hick accent would definitely stand out here.

"Matt?"

"Johnny." We embraced and I looked him over. The young man in his early twenties was gone. In his place an older more worn man stood. Johnny had been a man of average proportions, with a slight build that always reminded me more of a man who could lift things, but not run. He had a round and chubby face. He had gained weight since I last saw him, around his belly. Though his face, still white, still reddening, had lost most of its baby fat. There were more scars on his forehead, cheeks, and hands. His red shirt, and Hawaiian shorts, though, seemed to be the same ones I last saw him in.

"You look good, like you haven't changed a bit," he said, hand around my shoulder.

"Thanks." the compliment seemed to matter more to me than I had initially thought. "You don't look too shabby yourself."

He let out a laugh, his out loud chortle that definitely hadn't changed since the last time I saw him.

"Still the same Matt."

I slightly grinned, though I didn't know what he meant.

"Shitty neighborhood." He added as we walked back to my place. "Too many niggers."

I wasn't certain if he was asking or telling, especially since we hadn't seen anyone on the street, though I'm sure he could tell that once you get past 125th street, on any subway line, the cars get darker, browner and blacker. Fitted me, but I knew it didn't fit Johnny. I just hoped that he didn't use that word too loudly. Hard request to ask sometimes.

"I like it fine," I said, though it seemed to come out a little too tense.

"Ease up." He let out his chortle. "I'm just fucking with you. I actually have some business here in the Bronx. Good people."

Of course he would. His line of work. "Well keep that shit down in front of the old lady. She hears shit like that and it'll fuck things up between us. I don't need any more fights with her right now. She's already on edge about me leaving."

"Oh fuck, that's right. You going over *again*?"

I tilted my head slightly, trying to say it is what it is.

"You're one crazy bastard. You know that?"

We were in the elevator and I shrugged. I didn't have much else to say about the matter. I was patriotic. Not extremely, after all I got out, but enough to think that what I did still mattered to the overall safety of the country, of everyone in the country, of even the young woman in the elevator with us who had a surprisingly nice ass. "It's good money."

"So is what I do. Trust me on that. It's great money. You come work with me."

I shrugged again, as we walked out of the elevator and to my door. Johnny was smart, knew me pretty well, for as much as we had been apart, we were still very much alike. He was smart enough to use the word "with", and not "for", because my pride would rarely let me work *for* anyone, let alone a friend. Every job that I did, was done with gritted teeth.

"Hi honey." I opened the door to see her still on the same chair with the same book. "This is Johnny."

She got up from her chair and sauntered across the room. "Hi." She smiled a smile I hadn't seen since the first moments of our dating life. I missed that.

Johnny nodded. "Good to finally meet you. The woman who drove a nail through Matt's crazy years."

I grinned, some blood warming my face. It was never good to have separate parts of your life, where you lived like a different man, come together, you never knew what the combination would lead to. I had told the old lady a few stories, but nothing detailed, and none of the crazy stuff. I regretted not reminding Johnny to keep his mouth shut. Not that it would help, he seemed liquored enough not to care about what I said.

"Is that so?" My wife looked at me. "I'd like to hear all about that."

"Honey..." I glanced over at my friend. " Johnny, you need a drink?" I tried to shoot him a look that said shut the fuck up, but it might have been too subtle as the wife was examining my face.

"Sure thing."

I walked over to our kitchen and pulled out the tequila, his favorite drink, if I remembered correctly. "Tequila on the rocks?"

"Damn, still on the hard stuff, Matt?" He looked at me, and when I scowled. "That's fine."

"We have wine too," I said, wondering if Johnny had settled for drinking nothing but light beer for the end of his days.

The drinks were passed around and we chatted about the economic situation. Dire. America coming down. Could it ever come back up? We discussed the war on terror, though I talked about some of my friends still over there, staying away from what I had done in either of the wars. Funny how little people cared now that 9-11 was but another video slice amongst so many. My wife yawned.

"You want to go to sleep honey?"

"Yeah."

That meant the end of the night. In a place as small as ours, cozy with the two of us, crowded with three, the sofa only a few steps from the bed, the dining table between, one couldn't sleep without complete silence.

"Well it sounds like I should leave."

"You can stay," my wife offered, though I could tell, and I could tell Johnny could tell, it wasn't sincere.

"No, I should be going." He looked at his watch.

I instinctively looked at my watch, as if I would lose out on valuable information, and saw that it was 2am. He had arrived around 10. Time flies with a good friend. "I'll walk you out."

As we walked back to the station, the quiet that was the Bronx punctured by sirens, and a few people coming off late shifts meandering about the streets, filled me with sadness. I could feel something on Johnny 's mind invading the space between us. "You doing well?"

"Not too bad. I..." He looked about, as if thinking of a monster he would soon have to meet.

"What is it?" I tapped his shoulder lightly.

"Naw, just that I might be in some shit."

"What kind?"

"You know what I'm into, right?"

I felt weary about telling him not to do it. But what was a friend for? I thought back to what I used to think friendship was. The Army, the war, taught me that it could be so much more. Yet there had always been teachers and professors telling me that anyone who was involved with drugs—and that's what he was involved with—should be cut off, left to die, don't let them bring you down. What did those soft people know about friendship? They grew up in the 70s and 80s. All they knew or believed was money; the pill with which Christ was only the water to swallow it down with. How could I cut off this man in front of me, a man with whom I shared so much?

"How bad is it?"

"Bad."

"Can you get out? You can always just get a job somewhere, maybe go back to college."

He waved his hand at me. I stopped.

"That's a load of shit. I tried college, hated it. You know that. Couldn't stand those liberal fucks and all their whining. And you know I can't get a job, can't stand working for other people, it always ends up being a fight."

"Yeah," I said, thinking about how so many people like him would never fit into college because of traits they had learned, traits to be strong men, to be Americans, and when faced with something so foreign and against their culture, they simply threw their hands in the air and walked out, because they'll be damned if they say that their fathers and their fathers' fathers were full of shit. "I know. But I

20

managed it. Just hold your nose for a small while."

He shook his head. "I'm not you, I'm not you." He pulled out a cigarette, offered me one.

I took it. Had been five years since my last one, but I didn't want to drive a wedge between us; better to share the moment with some smoke than to never share it at all.

"She let you smoke?"

I laughed. "Fuck no. She'll kill me if she smells it, but I'm gonna write for some time and that should lighten the smell."

Johnny laughed out loud. Then he shook his head, looked off at some homeless man scurrying by us. The homeless man glanced at us, as if thinking of asking for money, then seemed to think better of it, and walked away.

"I'm gonna need your help."

I had figured as much, but I remained quiet as I wondered what that would entail. "It might have to wait. I leave pretty soon."

Johnny shook his head. "How do you do it?"

"What the work?"

"Yeah, going back over and over."

I wasn't certain what he was getting at, though I had an inkling that it was with the fact that, like many other Americans, Johnny hadn't served, never thought of serving and had to compensate for that by profusely thanking those who did. It always surprised me that so many people in a nation so proud were willing to step aside and let others do the dirty work of protecting them from the evil hordes of Muslims. "I'm contracting now, it's mainly for money. Nothing crazy. *Those* jobs are for the poor saps still in."

"It's the same, you're still risking your life."

"But the money is good. I should have enough to buy a new place once I'm done with this trip. And it'll be my last one."

Johnny blew out some smoke. "I'm glad to hear that, don't like hearing about you leaving all the time."

I weighed his words with a nod, wondering if he was trying to be nice; the words he spoke seemed sincere.

"What exactly are you into?" I asked, against my own judgment because I'd kept away from his illegal activities as a way to keep myself out of risk. Keep the old lady out of risk. But as with every moment before a deployment—even a deployment where the dangers were not going to be so bad—I felt the call of doing something outside the realm of my comfort zone; because at the end of the day the risks of being caught in a blast and biting it were higher than dying here in the Bronx.

"I started up my own business. We grow, we sell, we do everything."

"And someone wants in on your profits?"

"Exactly."

"Who?"

He looked me up and down. "Some group out of the valley. Bunch of Mexicans," he spat on the ground in disgust.

"Well pay them off."

"No fucking way some spics are going to get their hands on my money without me putting up a fight."

"How many men you got?"

"Five."

"Them?"

"I don't know, probably a hundred. You know how those wetbacks breed."

I blew out some air. I knew some Mexicans. One had paid his way across the border by carrying a bag full of drugs across the desert for hundreds of miles. Barely escaped with his life, and now he was a tax-paying worker. 140-hour weeks. Talk about the American dream. This Mexican friend hated gangs. I decided not to mention that to Johnny. "Then you're going to have a hell of a time battling them off."

"I was wondering if you could help."

"I said I have to go soon, Johnny, you know this." A NYPD squad car drove by and I wondered if they would deem us suspicious: a brown and white guy hanging out in the middle of the night in the Bronx. If they patted Johnny down I was certain he would spend the night, or longer, in jail. The smell of urine hit me and I looked over to see the homeless man, piss dribbling down his wet pants. The man looked familiar, I had seen him ask for money on the subway quite often. He was a black man, bald, and dreaded beard. He always caught my attention because he seemed well spoken.

"I know, but some advice maybe. After all, that was your job, right?"

"Fair enough. First, if they are more and you are less then you need to find ways to strike them, but not hard. Just wars of attrition. Have a safe area that they cannot penetrate, and you'll do fine. Lay traps, that whole thing. But finally, you must get some sort of political compromise, there's nothing without it, because they are more than you, and unless you plan on killing hundreds of men..." I looked at him, and wondered how many men he had killed so far. It wasn't an easy business, but one thing the cops hated was bodies showing up. Lessons learned: they couldn't touch the gangs in LA, but they at least warned them that if bodies showed up they would start hammering down on them.

"I'll do that before I give some spics my hard-earned money," muttered Johnny.

"Very well, then find names and houses and snatch them one by one, and never make noise about it." I gave the advice with more confidence than I should have. I had experience advising foreign groups on how to wage war, or counter-insurgency, or counter terrorism, but how would that help Johnny?

Johnny nodded his head thoughtfully. Did he know whether what I said made sense? Was it just my wartime experience that made him think it would all be worthy of consideration? He had lived the drug life longer than I, and one thing I knew is that on the ground experience beat most everything else.

We stood there, the homeless man walked past us again, hardly giving us a look. I noticed that he didn't have any shoes on, and his feet, powdered in white, gave off a horrendous stench, like rotten vomit. A siren went off in the distance. A pair of large white men, with crooked noses walked out of the subway. The look they gave us was one of carefree apathy mixed with hints of violence. I nodded at them, but they just stared at me.

"Your wife is nice, by the way."

"Thanks. I rcally do." I figured the l-word was too much to use. "Care for her. She's been the best."

"I can see. Ol' Matt completely domesticated. Never thought I would see the day."

"And yourself? Any women you've taken a liking to?"

"Fuck no." He threw his cigarette down the subway stairs. "Just hookers for me. I can't stand bitches and their complaints anymore."

I nodded my head, and wondered when I had lost the attitude he had. Was it when I decided to settle down, or quit, or give up, or finally be accepted by society? "Well you do what you gotta do."

Johnny nodded. "By the way, thanks man, and take care. Call me when you get back. All right?"

I nodded my head. "Of course, take care of yourself. And..." I threw my cigarette down on the ground. "Don't do anything drastic. I'll be back, then I can help you out."

We embraced and I watched as he walked down the stairs. I hoped that he wouldn't get into trouble, but with the game that he played, he wouldn't have much room to maneuver to stay out of trouble. I had other friends like him, proud young men who had long given up dreams they had no right to hold, and settled with demeaning jobs so they could continue a meek existence. Johnny just wasn't willing to go that route.

I turned to walk back to the apartment, in front of the stoops of a tall brick building the two white men, most likely Eastern European of some kind, were conversing with two Dominican-looking men. They all stopped as I passed by, staring at me, with a slight distaste on all of their mouths.

My heart jumped. I wondered if they were thinking of jumping me; no one was on the streets. I stared back, holding the shank I had hidden in my pocket. Perhaps I never really recovered from the war. Not that I had been through anything like Barbarossa, but the twitches were still there; the need to have a weapon, the need to see enemies in every movement, make sure you're not caught off guard. Old girlfriend, while I was in the Army, told me that I was too twitchy for her liking, or rather I'd spoil great 'alone' moments because of the way I kept darting my head, certain that an ambush was coming. She was fun. Fucked like a whore on coke.

In some bushes I heard a rustle and could see the homeless man stretching out for some sleep. I wondered if I could ever be like that, sad and angry at society, so much that I refused to participate in an acceptable way. But wasn't that what this man was doing? If he truly hated the people of the world why didn't he move to Alaska? Or some other sparsely populated part of the country. I could smell him as I walked past him, the summer air allowing the smell to grow and stretch out. What a City, I would be glad to get out of it for a break.

As I made my way to my building, I thought of the semi-promise I made for Johnny. Would I help when I came back? Did I really mean it? Doing so would immediately sacrifice my life with the wife. The domestication of Matt would be over. Was I willing to give that up? In truth I had some voice deep inside telling me not do this, not get the corporate job that I was planning on getting, and not settle down completely. Is that what the promise was about? It couldn't be, if it was only a matter of moving or not wanting to settle I could travel for a while and be fine. What I had promised Johnny was that I would be willing to break the law alongside him. That was basically a death warrant. Especially in the drug game.

I opened the door to my place; the old lady sat up from underneath the sheets. I knew then that Johnny would have to wait, that I would have to find a way to weasel out of my promise to him. I couldn't give up this woman of mine.

"He was an interesting guy," she said.

I took off my shoes and lay down next to her. She must have had a quick shower because she smelled clean, fresh, good enough to eat out again. I nuzzled my nose into her neck, kissed her, tasted the clean skin, sweet like the first time we nibbled on each other.

"That he is."

"What does he do?"

The big question.

The old lady was never good with the shady side of life. She was a professional to the heart. Did perfect in school, better in grad school, then performed flawlessly at work. The idea of even doing wrong was anathema to her and her ilk... the rich serfs of the new world. Here's your village, don't disobey and you'll be allowed to live.

Tell you the truth I liked that, enjoyed the serenity it provided. And yet after all I had been through, I knew it as something that may have been good for her, her health, mine too, but it required blinders to live with in this manner in complete contentment. In the end, I loved her for it.

"A lot of odd jobs. Construction here and there." I kissed her back. What else was I going to say?

"That sounds like you're holding something from me." She tapped my cock.

I wondered if she could tell. Give it a few years of cohabitation and someone should be able to tell anything, shouldn't they? We are limited organisms, whatever else we would like to think, and that means there is only so much to learn.

"I'm not, baby. Don't be ridiculous." I thought of the next few days. I would get a call and fly out soon. I wanted to see Jenny. Not for anything but the release that she provided. "I'll have to go and finish some training the next few days. All right?"

She hesitated. "Oh?"

"Yes, I'll see you before I go, though."

"Why thank you."

I sucked in some air through my teeth. Couldn't leave on a trip overseas with something between us. "Baby, you know I have to do this. And it's the last time. Well for the trip, at least."

"I know," she said, in a voice that gave hints that she didn't in fact know, or rather that she felt completely wronged.

She turned, her face resting where my chest and shoulder met. She fell asleep. Her cute snoring started, and she twitched, and I slowly pulled away from her. There was a seed of a story that I had to plant onto my computer.

When I was done typing, I looked over at the old lady. She was sprawled out on our bed, beautiful as ever. I could never believe that I found her. I looked at my email. Jenny had written.

When can I see you next?

Tomorrow, I'll give you a call.

I'd see her for one day, release my inhibitions, then spend the rest of my time with the old lady. That way, things would be good on all fronts for when I returned.

*

"Hi." Jenny nuzzled on my neck. We were in the basement of a bookstore in Soho. I looked around, trying to see if anyone was watching. As much as I wanted to be with Jenny, I missed the wife, felt guilty for leaving her for some fling. But I was a man, wasn't I? I looked Jenny up and down again. There was too much to like with her body. I grabbed her waist and pulled her in closer.

"Shall we go to your place?" I kissed her collarbone. She smelled like a bouquet of flowers—slightly different from last time—her perfume was expensive enough to be so subtle, the smell was almost a dream. The time it took her to answer let me know that there was something on her mind. Was she going to ask what the relationship was leading to? I had her pegged for a woman who didn't care much about what other lives I lived.

"Okay." She pulled away, a slight coldness enveloped her demeanor, she was treating me like a stranger.

"Something the matter?"

"No, nothing."

Terse, too quickly answered. Christ, when would I find respite from women like these? I paused to look at a book section as we walked upstairs. Javier, a favorite author of mine from Spain. I pointed it out to her.

She gave the one I pointed out a look, took a glance and grabbed it. I followed her to the cashier's desk. I took another glance at her body. She was wearing a skirt with a combination tube top and shirt with dangling frills that looked like it fit in around Soho. Though less revealing than normal, her curves and thighs still jutted out and tickled my groin.

We walked the entire way to her apartment without speaking a word. Since she seemed content to stare at buildings she must have seen a hundred times before, I spent my time watching the people who walked by. The tourists scattered between seemed to stand out like rocks in a stream, City people gushing by them, some with evil stares, others as if this was to be expected. One thing that this city could provide was a collage of faces—in Soho that meant shiny sharp faces of generic beauty—but in addition to that it could provide the pleasant surprise of futuristic mixed faces: dark skin and light eyes.

She managed not to look at me the entire walk. I wondered if she was angry, but once we got to her place, she placed her bags on the table, and threw her shoes across her living room. The place seemed to ring with a familiarity that I enjoyed; it didn't yet feel old. I examined her as she, her back to me, took off her shirt and her tube top remained. For a second I thought about my wife and how she wanted to see me one more time. An enormous weight pushed on my heart, slowing it down.

Jenny turned to me and smiled, one foot flexed in front of the other, lifting up her skirt. I was a man, wasn't I? I fucked her in proper   don't-give-a-fuck-there-might-not-be-a-tomorrow-pre-deployment-mentality style.

Once my mind was washed through, I lay back on the bed and let out a cloud of air.

She smiled at me, looked at me and seemed to know what I was thinking.

"So what is it that you do?"

Of course she would ask such a thing. She was a smart one. Still, I couldn't spill the beans to just any woman. I even kept the old lady in the dark for the most part, though that was to protect her from anxiety. "I told you."

"You deflected it with some cool ass story." She twirled her finger on my forearm, giving me a haughty look. "But you didn't answer me with a specific job. Consulting? Are you a spy?"

Not a question I liked, even though what I did was nothing that a spy did. I smiled, though I didn't want to. "Don't be ridiculous. Of course not." I looked away, then decided that it would be best to look her in her eyes. She seemed especially full of life.

"Oh no? I think that's what a spy would say."

I chortled. "Is that a fact? Are you a spy?"

She burst out laughing and jumped on top of me, pretending to fight, devolved into kissing, and then another romp within the sheets.

After we were done, she lay with her head on the nook between my shoulder and chest.

"I'll be leaving for a while, for another overseas job, all right?"

She seemed startled, took a deep swig of air to regain some of her composure. "Sure thing. When will you be back?"

"A few months. Don't call my number, I'll email you when I get back, all right?"

"From your place in Harlem?" she said coldly.

Perhaps she had figured out that part of the story I had told her was bullshit, but I had to assume that she hadn't, that she was currently relying on a few strands tainted with the possibility of bullshit and I couldn't slip anymore, could only run with what I had. I shook my head. "Don't be ridiculous. I'll just be gone for a while."

For the briefest of seconds, the image of my wife, lying next to me drifted into my head; the feeling of having her calming presence next to me, her smell soaked into my every pore and forced me to stop and think if I should tell Jenny that I was married. That could complicate things immensely. On one hand, after a few more hours I wouldn't have much use for her, except to do some damage control to have something for when I came back. On the other hand if I told her and she suddenly became vindictive—and one can never really tell which woman is going to blame herself, going to be French about the whole thing and shrug it off, or going to be a moralizing and revenge-driven unholy bitch and set plans to destroy what I had with my wife—and decided that she would indeed call my place, or find out where I lived and cause problems for my old lady. That I didn't need. And yet if I didn't tell her and she decided to become worried and call my wife incessantly, what would I do?

I rubbed her thigh, still a perfect specimen of aphrodisiacal ability, and took in her room. I would miss her, that was for certain. There was a certain quality in her that I loved, that filled me with energy and made me enjoy her presence, more than just her physical appearance could provide on its own. Behind her cold efficiency was a gentle, loving heart, which seemed to reach inside me. In a city full of gorgeous women that was saying something. I would have to trend carefully if I was to keep her.

"Do you understand?" I asked, even though there had been too long a pause between my two statements.

She tilted her head as if to say maybe and she rolled out of bed, slipping into a bathrobe. "You want something to eat?"

"Yeah. I'll help." I stepped out of bed, put on my pants, and walked with her to the kitchen. I hadn't truly examined it the last time. I saw the usual college-aged magnetic words on her fridge and everything else, the espresso machine, the mixer, were tainted with what looked like German steel. It gave the place the same efficient feeling that she evoked upon first glance.

I helped her bake a frozen pizza. Again she was quiet. I could've let it fester or I could've dealt with it at that moment.

I preferred to delay it, and ate my pizza, enjoying the silence. One thing about pre-deployments, even if they aren't going to be memorable, is that you need to stock up on memories for the slower moments when you're away from everyone. This was one such moment.

When I finished my pizza I leaned back from my chair to look at Jenny. I could see that her face was on the verge of breaking. Into what was the question. She could very well surprise me and hold it all in and just ask me to leave.

My phone vibrated and I pulled out of my pocket. The wife had texted me.

We need to talk, now.

This was really the last thing I wanted. Two issues with two different women. Why was the world so cruel?

"Who is that?"

The wife, I considered saying, but knew that it would be a certain way to get kicked out. I would have to leak out the information to her slowly. I could feel my heart beat faster, sweat dripped from my armpits; I moved my arms. Did I really care about her this much after so little had transpired?

"Why?"

Again that startled look on her face, like she had never been asked such a question, like she had never been handled with this emotional toughness before in her life.

Silence.

"If you don't want to say, you don't have to. I just thought," she trailed off to think more, and in those moments I could see her toughen up into the City-girl I thought I saw that first time in a café.

"Listen." I took her hand in mine. "You know I think you're an amazing woman." I got off my seat and came closer to her. A small tug and she got up off her seat; her robe half-opened and exposed her body. I felt her breasts against the top of my stomach, and held her by her upper arms. "Right?"

She nodded, a small smile on her lips. I could see that she had indeed decided to toughen up; perhaps she could take anything that I sent her way. "What are your thoughts on, on us?"

She shrugged, avoided my gaze for a second, looked at me. "I think you're amazing too. I like what we have here."

There was something in the way she spoke, the way she seemed to have a mask that caught me off guard for a moment. Who was leading who here? No, I thought, she was toughened from the City but nothing more. "I do too. But what do you expect from us?"

"Fun," she said in a way that almost turned it into a question.

Something about her was measured. Then she returned to being out of her element. "Good," I said, as if it would cement what we had just talked about.

The rest of the time with her was spent without a hitch. I enjoyed her body, and we talked about some art books she had. We both shared a love for Rodin and we discussed what happened with Camille. Rodin's protégé who carried out an illicit affair with him, only to have him spurn her for his old trustworthy wife. She lost her sense of being after that, though not before creating some amazing pieces. My favorite was one with an old man being taken by an old woman, a young docile girl on her knees behind them.

"The Rodin museum is one of my favorite places in Paris."

"Me too." She smiled and pushed herself closer to me on the couch.

"You think Rodin did her wrong?"

"No, she was a grown woman, she knew what she was getting into."

I liked hearing that, and I guided the conversation to some of Rodin's more memorable pieces, like the muse. After that we discussed Paris and made semi-plans to visit it.

"I have a little party I have to stop by for a short moment. You want to come with?"

I looked at my watch and decided to go with her, if only to grease the wheels for our next visit.

At the party she introduced me to a man or boy she seemed to know. He was a typical village male: white, with a hat and sunglasses on indoors, preppy linen jacket and limp demeanor.

"Matt." I shook hands with him.

"James." He shook my hand. "What is it you do?"

Did I have time for a full explanation? "Write. You?"

"Same here." He nodded with some approval. "What is it you write?"

"Thrillers."

"Good. Good," he said, though I could tell that he did not care for genre fiction.

"And you?"

"I write in some literary magazines, finishing a novel right now."

"Oh?" I scrunched up my chin. Someone finishing at least one novel was no easy feat. "What's it about?"

"The City, life here is fascinating, you know?"

"I agree. What facet of the City are you looking at?"

"How writers survive."

I paused, it sounded like something I tended to avoid like the Ebola virus. But I decided to let him have a chance. "The story?"

"No story, no plot. Plots are so tired. You know?"

I game a non-committed tilt of my hands and body.

"Well I definitely think that. Why stick to same thing that has been done before? That's why I write without those constrictions."

"Fair enough. So what is it about?"

"A writer, his struggle to get published and the things he does in the City. You know, restaurants he eats at, the people he meets, his thoughts, wandering the street, the trials of not fitting in perfectly. Intellectual stuff."

"Well I'm sure it will be well received."

I eyed the door and figured I had to leave. Some people in the City sapped my goodwill to mankind to no end. Jenny swooped in behind me just in time. We made out in the hallway for a few minutes. Then I went into the bathroom and rinsed off her lipstick.

And with that I bid her good bye:

"Oh yes, your secret job."

I laughed. "I'll send postcard, all right?"

She smiled. "I would like that."

I made it back to my wife as quickly as possible, happy that Jenny was in the bag. One thing being on a special ops team taught you was to separate the side-women from the heart. I thought I had done that fairly well with Jenny. "Hi, honey, I came back as soon as I could," I said as I walked in.

She was sitting on the sofa reading the same book as before.

"What took you so long?"

"Nothing, I told you I was training."

She looked at me without replying. I took off my shoes and sat next to her.

"Well babe?" I placed my hand on her knee, trying to see what was in her eyes. They seemed more placid than normal.

"I'm pregnant."

"Oh." I tried to think, then smiled, then remembered that I should be a little more excited. We hadn't really made plans, but we'd talked about it enough. "That's great honey." I moved in for a hug. "When did you find out?"

"Today. You remember my doctor's appointment, right?"

"Right," I said, though I was certain that she had never mentioned it, it was best to go with the flow rather than argue with her. I felt like an ass for delaying coming back to her for so long.

She sniffed near me. "You smell like perfume."

Oh shit.

"Oh that." I waved my hand into the air. "I had to drop into a small party with some hobnobbing of the boss and some clients. For the next job."

She bit her lower lip like the story sufficed for now.

I knew I would have to remember to be more careful next time.

We spent the rest of the night making preparations for our future together. A great moment, as I realized that I was fine with

Nelson Lowhim

living with the old lady for the rest of my life.

A couple of days later I left for Amman. There, at the embassy, I ran into my old friend Joe, an easygoing fellow who, except for his southern accent, always reminded me of a surfer. He had a blond mop, lanky limbs, and rarely had a look of concern on his face. We met years ago in the Q-course, running exhausting patrols and laughing at the cadre whenever their backs were turned. We had managed to stay in touch throughout the years as he shifted his work more and more into the dark side, while I was winding it down.

"Matt." He patted me on my back as I waited to meet with the officer in charge of my mission. "Good to see you."

I cracked a grin; it did feel good to see him, like the good times of the Army were tied to him. "You too." I pointed at the seat next to me.

"You're gonna see the boss next?"

"That's what they tell me." I didn't want to say it, but this trip, unlike the multiple ones before it, was pulling at my nerves. I knew I would have to go out to the borderlands of Afghanistan, and though I'd seen my share of action before, this time I was apprehensive about it. I couldn't place the reason. Was it the old lady's tearful—more so than ever before—good-bye? Was it the fact that she was pregnant and I was about to be a father? I was getting soft with age. The money, the money for this was good, and would help set my child's future. "Yeah, you?"

"You're gonna be working with me." Joe gave a big smile.

I smiled back and felt some tension leave my body. This would be better. It was always hard going on a mission with people you didn't know. A mutual friend of ours had a contracting trip to

Afghanistan a few months ago and when I talked to him he complained about having to baby-sit recon and ranger guys. He had a hell of a time and though he got a job to come back, he felt like he had to rely on people he hated. My last experience contracting hadn't been too bad, had to look after some local soldiers, jundees, in the UAE. At least the time off there wasn't too bad; I got to like Abu Dhabi.

"Great, where are we headed first?"

A few days of preparation and we headed out to Afghanistan with a simple enough mission. Tried to infiltrate some of the ratlines that led from Pakistan to Afghanistan. Our compound was at the foot of some horrendously gray and brown looking mountains. The wind whipped up and down their slopes like a terrible omen trying to drive away all who dared to visit. The compound itself had a few concrete buildings with large concrete barriers around them, and several trailers, our living quarters, also surrounded by concrete barriers and sandbag roofs. We had some Afghan Army soldiers guarding our one entrance, the entire wall being made of the same concrete barriers as well as concertina wire. It was like every military compound in Iraq or Afghanistan that I had seen. There was an ODA nearby and we got to know them pretty well, traded whiskey with them, as they ended up being our hands on the field most of the time.

Joe was on edge since we were on the same compound where a suicide bomber, supposedly working for us, had blown up a few of the men. He always double-checked the perimeter every night. And for all those nerves, everything he did was gold. He knew exactly what to do, how to ask the local tribesmen how to help, then picking out the weak amongst them to come over to our side. It was his fifth time doing this particular job.

One night we celebrated finding some large caches by drinking a few rounds of scotch.

"Five times, huh?"

"Yeah, getting pretty good at this." He took a sip from his tumbler.

I nodded, felt guilty, perhaps even jealous. I was once as gung-ho as he was. "Better man than I." I tried to delve into my own mind to find out why I didn't care to do this anymore. There were some things here that I would never be able to mimic back home. Was that it? I was too soft, old, and wanted an easy life? "How do you do it?" I took a sip of my scotch, let the harsh, almost revolting liquid settle on my tongue, numb it, then flow down my throat. I felt better.

"Come on, you're doing it right now."

I shook my head. "I've only come over a couple times since I left the military. And this is my last trip. After this it's the easy stuff stateside that I'll deal with."

He paused, took another sip. "More than what most people do."

I took the comment with a grain of salt, as I had no idea if it was meant to be a good or bad thing. Then again, I knew Joe didn't have a resentful bone in his body.

"Maybe. But I know that I'm done doing it."

"I'm sure you'll be fine either way," Joe said. We didn't talk for the night. Finished our drinks and went to sleep.

Two days later a mortar landed next to Joe and he died. I watched as he was flown out. His body and face a mangled mess.

The next night I went out with the ODA, the people who had a hand in the mortar were supposedly in a compound. We surrounded it. I tensed up next to a Humvee. I was to run inside with the team. I was glad they were allowing this. Everyone in the house surrendered, and I was slightly annoyed that no one wanted to fight. We found mortars, though the family claimed that it was from guests who had left the night before. We handed over the military aged men to the ODA so they could deal with them. I wasn't certain they were guilty, and even if they were... I tried to cut off that line of thinking. Still it was the current and past rule that we consider guilty any military aged male within a neighborhood of a crime. And yet I could only think of Joe.

After that, I could barely face my job. The only thing that drove me to do well was the man who replaced Joe was a complete asshole, but still someone who needed my help. He was Texan and kept emphasizing that, especially when he seemed confused. Half of me wanted to watch him fuck up, maybe even die, the other half knew it would be bad to let down the war effort, even if it meant helping him. I was further inflamed with how he always kept invoking how great it was to do the work of a nation. As if it was a pep speech that would help me along. "We're the ones sacrificing, right?" he said one day. My hasty glance his way seemed to shut him up, but only for a while.

The day I left the Texan, Tim, came up to me as I gathered all my gear and waited for the helicopter to come by.

"Matt." He seemed flustered, red with emotion. "I just want to say, thank you for all you've done here. I will make sure higher knows all about your work here." He searched my face for a sign of some sort.

I stayed quiet; observing without a single trace of emotion, I really didn't care for him, and I thought my aloof actions had led him to the same conclusion.

"You'll always have a job around here. Or anywhere." He squinted at the distant speck that was the chopper in the horizon. "I know you took the loss of Joe hard, and my words don't mean as much, but everything you did was appreciated. Not many men would have gone on." He stuck out his hand.

I looked at it for a second. Did he have any idea how much I would have loved to smack him? He was overweight, which was another thing that annoyed me. Only a part of me felt stroked by his words; the rest of me didn't want to feel that. I shook his hands.

He turned to walk away.

"Tim."

He turned when I spoke, his face eager for some words.

"Take care of yourself here. All right?"

"I will." He nodded solemnly, as if my words hid kernels of lost sagacity.

He walked away and the helicopter got closer. I was done with this place and the likes of Tim. I felt slightly elated that Tim said he would recommend me for another job, or, it seemed, a job of my choice. That would help my pay. Then I felt disgusted with myself for ever thinking in such terms.

On the ride out, I watched the peaks of the hills race by. Part of me was looking forward to seeing the old lady again. I had emailed her constantly until Joe died. Then I had sent only sent the email telling her I was coming back. I wondered what Jenny was doing, and if she would still care to see me. Inside my stomach a cold bubble formed for Joe, his wife and kids; they missed out on one more homecoming.

*

When I saw the old lady, a slight bump had formed on her belly. I kissed her, held her like her body so close to mine was some balm. She never questioned me about why I hadn't emailed. Back home, I held and kissed her all over her body. Tasting, licking, enjoying just being near her. I had never felt such a sense of desire and togetherness before—like our hearts had melded together. On a level it frightened me because it felt like I was losing control. And what woman wants a man like that?

We spent an entire week in each other's arms, exploring, asking questions that I hadn't thought to ask since the first years of our relationship. At one point I wanted to talk to her about Joe, and how I still seemed to lose myself in the memory of his death. How it didn't seem right not to do something about it, and yet I was at a loss for what that would entail. A part of me wanted to watch people, not just the perpetrators, but people in general, suffer for the incident. It wasn't a comfortable thought.

I never once had an image of Jenny pop into my head during this time.

Later I went to the offices of a company that was located on Fifth Avenue in Midtown. They had an immediate security job for me, and it paid over a thousand dollars a day. I couldn't complain. The man who gave me the job, head of security, seemed a little full of himself. I didn't like him, smelled too much like the crappy officers I knew in the regular Army. His suit was worn with an excessive pride, as was his high and tight haircut. The sight of both those things made me want to walk out, but we needed the money, so I decided to bear and grin it.

"You've done this kind of thing before?" He looked me up and down.

"Yes." Normally I would have said something snappy to him. I looked through the file with a picture of a man, as well as his entourage. "Basic surveillance, right?"

He nodded, more thoughtfully than was required. "You will have to get a photo of him doing anything illegal, as well as meeting with him." He pointed at another man's photo.

"Do I get a team?"

He looked me up and down. "No, can you handle this by yourself? If not..."

He trailed off. I let out a lungful of air. This moron was trying to browbeat me into a foolish surveillance mission. So be it; if they wanted shoddy work from one man, and my experience told me that one man would never be enough, even if he was super man, then that's what I would give them. "Where are my tools?"

"You'll get all that you need."

I thought for another second. What was this moron's deal? Half of me wanted to storm out. I sized him up again. Definitely regular Army. Someone who was not used to doing anything but exerting control over his men. He needed, nay required, being barked at. I'd dealt with these kinds of people before, I just hoped I'd left them behind in the Army. "What kind of fucking scheme are you running here? I'll get what I need? Let me see the fucking tools, then I'll tell you what else I need. Got it?" I raised my voice for the last part, stepping towards him like I was ready to strike him.

He flinched. He hadn't expected it. "Got it. We'll take you to see the surveillance room. Can you start now?"

"Sure, give me a couple hours."

I waited for the secretary, some hot twenty-something with perky tits-ass and a robot-perfect face, and a tight blue business suit, who led me to the room. It was aptly named. Filled with camera jacket, bags, bugged phones, telescopic cameras, GPS bugs and even keys to cars that I would need. I grabbed several cars, jackets, bags, phones, watches and other goodies. It was enough to make Mr. Bond cry.

I looked up the file again. On the smartphone they gave me, I marked the places he visited, examined the street-views of where he lived so I knew which buildings had the best view of his offices and rooms. He was a bigwig businessman, and didn't seem to have much illegal interests, but it wasn't my place to wonder what he had done wrong, and just get paid. I had a baby on the way, I reminded myself, there were bigger things in life than mere ideals.

The icy moron came back when I had packed a car full of goodies.

"Where do you think you're going?"

"Getting the job done. What the fuck are you doing?" I pointed at a bag. "Throw that in the back." I double checked all the cameras in the car, and the other four cars, made sure their GPS was working then turned to the man who had put the bag in the trunk only with great deliberation.

"You planning on coming with me?" I asked him still making sure that my voice was low and angry, he wasn't going to get any slack from me. "Because if so, you're going to have to change out of that ill-fitting suit." I remembered that I really hated officers. "Where were you, the 82nd?"

"Yes." He puffed out his chest. "I was, you?"

"Hell no. Did you come down here to tell me that?" I was surprised that he hadn't done a rudimentary check on my background. I thought he would at least have some motivation to do extra work. Now it seemed the company would only keep someone like him around because he looked dependable, and one to keep his mouth shut. Traits from his previous work.

"No." He pondered something, looking at all the cars and gear that I had snatched up. "Are you going to need all this?"

I cocked my head at him. "Are you fucking serious? Am I not alone?"

He shrugged.

"Am I, or am I not? You see, because if I am then I'm going to need all this shit just to keep up with a guy who has a security detachment. Got it?"

He nodded, again slightly perturbed, but something still seemed to bother him.

"Have you ever done this before?"

"Yes."

"No, not sat around while others did it, but have you actually done this before?"

"No," he murmured.

41

"Good, then you'll know to stay out of my way." With that last word, I decided to stop. I might have been taking it too far. His demeanor didn't seem to warrant my outburst, and I could very well end up without a job. Was it the fact that someone like Joe had died, while this douchebag in front of me had survived? No, even with the old lady I had been silent and brooding. Every time I wanted to tell her what was on my mind, I held back, because I didn't want her to suffer with me. Perhaps this man would be my piñata.

"Listen," he said, his voice retaining its earlier bravado. "I'm in charge here, so you have to tell me where you are at all times. Got it?"

"All times? Are you serious? How do you expect me to get any work done?"

"You're not the only one working for us. So we have to make certain that there aren't any unnecessary clashes."

"Clashes? Where are we, Baghdad?"

He looked over my bags again. "And bring everything back."

I looked him up and down; he wasn't that big, most of his muscle was in his arms, his back and hips held no weight. He looked easily stoppable. Nothing in the world would have made me happier than to cut into him, but I decided to hold back. "Of course Patton. What, did you think I was going to make for the hills with this gear?"

"You have almost a million dollars worth of gear," he said, as if that was enough.

"Got it. Don't steal. How about murder?"

He fumed through his nose. "I'll expect a report by tomorrow."

"No, by the day after. I'm supposed to tail him for ten hours today, correct?"

"That's right."

I left it at that. He paused as if he wanted to say one more thing, then turned to walk away.

"Another thing," I called out to him.

"What," he asked testily as he glared over his shoulder.

"I need cash and a credit card."

"What?"

"Yes, to help me access buildings here and there." I pointed at my watch. "He moves in an hour, so there isn't much time to argue."

He chortled—the first time I'd seen him smile—and shook his head. He reached into his pocket and pulled out some cash, and a credit card. "Here you go."

I grabbed the money and squealed out in a car. There were four main areas this man worked. I parked each car within a few blocks of these places. Each car had a change of clothes, disguises, cameras that I could use at the last minute. The last vehicle, a small van with all the telecommunications equipment, was kept in the center.

Nearby I found homeless men who seemed to be legitimate and asked them if they wanted to make a quick buck.

Of course.

I had them wait nearby after giving them each a twenty. It would come into handy for later. Normally, one was given more time to case the areas, but I would have to make do.

I waited outside his office building near Penn Station. When he came out, two guards behind him, I knew who it was from his large pot-bellied body and power-manual saunter. I followed far behind. It was easy to follow those two large bodyguards of his, they were each at least six-five. They went into a building that I had marked as a place of residence.

I walked in and saw him disappear into an elevator.

"Can I help you sir?" The doorman offered me a suspicious but friendly smile.

I glanced at the list of company names with suites on the wall. "Yes, I was looking for Maria Gomez with the Florez Consulting Company? I'm late." I looked at my watch. "Which floor?"

"Very well sir, we have a sign up sheet here."

I jotted down a fake name, pretending to be in a rush and walked to the elevator before he could say anything else. In the elevator I slipped on a pair of camera glasses and waited.

As soon as the door opened to the floor I saw him staring right at me. My heart gasped, and I barely kept my presence of mind to press the button in my pocket and take photos of him. I walked

43

out and waited until the door was closed before I looked at the elevator numbers. He had left the building. By the time I got back down he was gone.

This is why you need a team, I reminded myself.

I rushed to the other building that he was known to do business in. I had to get some sort of GPS tracking device on him, or else all was lost. I couldn't stand the thought of being ridiculed by that officer in charge of security.

The lobby here was much stricter about who they let in. I walked out. The building across, and from which I would be provided a good angle of the target's room, had a similar rule: no one was let in unless accompanied, or phoned in by someone in the building. I walked over to the homeless man I'd talked to earlier.

"Wanna earn a hundred bucks?"

"What do I have to do?" The homeless guy eyed me suspiciously.

"Run into that building." I pointed at the building that was across from where the target might have been. "And make a ruckus. Ten minutes gets you hundred. Meet me back here afterwards and I'll give you all the money."

He glanced down at a meal he had just started.

"Give me an answer now, or else I'll go somewhere else with my money."

"Okay." He lumbered off his patch of ground with wet, dirty cardboard laid down, and a bag that was black with dirt. "Money first." He held his hand out.

Now that he was up, I could smell his feet and urine, cooked in the summer sun. I held myself back from dry heaving. "Twenty now." I pulled out a bill, "more later. Got it?"

He grabbed the money, grunted, gathered the bag and without a word walked off to the building. I followed after a minute.

Inside he was already standing on the lobby desk, his bag's innards strewn all over the floor, his stench had already overpowered all the ACed air and the security men were approaching him with hands over their mouths and noses, scared of touching him.

I walked into the elevator and up to the 13th floor. It was a series of residences, so I looked for cameras. None. I knocked on the doors on the side I wanted.

"Yes?" an old lady said from behind a door.

"Is Maria Lopez here?"

"No one here by that name."

"Sorry."

I walked to the next one, knocked. Nothing. Knocked again, still nothing.

I looked back and forth and could feel sweat on my hands. I pulled out the blank key that I had. I fitted it into the keyhole and banged it through. With a slight turn the door opened. I walked side. It was a clean apartment with stylish minimalist modern furniture, leather surfaces, and a white carpet. I walked carefully to the wide bay window. I counted the windows on the building across the street. That should have been his. There was a balcony, but I couldn't be seen so I pulled the curtains and pulled out my camera. I zoomed in on his window. There was a reflection from the sun, but I could see his body shape inside, talking to a man with four stars. I zoomed in further and started taking pictures.

I had some listening devices and started to record. It was hard to hear them, but a few words came through. Another general giving up another contract for a friend who used to be a general. I felt nauseous but held it down.

"Perfect, perfect." The officer, named Smith, was looking through my report and pictures. "Good job." He stared with approval.

I didn't care for the man, but it felt good to hear that. Especially after all I had been through. My arms still felt like they had been pulled from their sockets. I groaned. "Thanks."

"We pay extra for good work, so know that you'll be taken care of, I'll make certain of that. All right?"

I didn't want to look surprised. "Thanks."

"I read your background."

I sensed some awe somewhere in there.

I felt like a moron for being so harsh on him before.

"Your arms okay?"

"Give me a week." I grimaced as I tried to move them. Nothing was broken, but I would have to rest them.

After I had taken the photos, the target had left and I packed my gear into my bag only to hear the lock turn on the door. I ran out to the balcony and jumped over the ledge, turning to grab a hold of it. It was cement-based, and I didn't have any gloves on. I fell to the next one. And then the next one. Each time my skin scraped off and my arms, at first not feeling too bad, began to scream at the amount they had to grab. By the fifth one I decided to try and land on my feet, but almost toppling over caused me to rethink that. Twenty minutes later I landed on the awning for the lobby. I lay on top of it until I felt I could move again.

I met up with the homeless man after that, and he was smiling, his teeth yellow on the edges, his eyes a startling greenish blue. I smiled back and handed him the money. You are a crazy bastard, aren't you? I looked him up and down. He was large, maybe 200pounds, and barrel chested. Perhaps, I would say, he ate too much. Odd. He was mixed, for certain, he had a tan skin that could have been comfortable in any trader's isle in the world. Thank you, we'll stay in touch. That we will.

I followed the target again.

I got a few more pictures of him, but nothing else. I would need more time to penetrate the cloak of secrecy he had around him.

"We'll give you a call next week then?"

"Will I get my team?"

Smith smiled. "Of course, you've earned it."

That made me feel good.

*

As I entered the lobby I called my wife. "Honey I should be home soon. Work was... tough." When I hung up I felt a tap on my shoulder. I turned.

It was Jenny.

"Hi honey," she said in a mocking tone. Then she wagged her finger at me. "You said you would call." She tilted her head ever so slightly.

I couldn't detect a hint of hurt in her tone, so I decided that she was playing. "Sorry, been busy, and only got back last week." I could smell her perfume, slightly different than last time, this one had the mix of an exotic bazaar with hints of artic flowers, it was spellbinding and I was immediately hooked. No, I was trying to be good. My old lady was pregnant and waiting for me. Another look up and down her body, the curves where they should have been, her thighs proudly shining underneath her skirt, made me forget about the wife. It was fall, but warm enough that she had another skimpy jacket on.

"That's the best you can do?"

I looked away. Desire was building up, but I couldn't lie to her for it. Not straight away at least. It surprised that behind that physical desire there was a part of me that missed her smile, laugh, the cuddling.

"Who was that? The ball and chain?" She grabbed the cuff on my rolled up sleeves. Touched my forearm and I felt a jolt.

"The wife. I'm married."

"Oh no." She opened her eyes wide and covered her mouth. Then she broke out into a smile.

I felt out of place, almost a pawn. The Jenny I knew from before was not this manipulative and playful, or was she? Was that the reason I had decided to avoid her?

"Well..." I trailed off. I was at a loss for words, wondering what to say about the colliding voices in my head. She would be the perfect release.

"Are you nervous?" she said, still teasing, and she let out that laugh and I knew then that I had missed it.

"No." I regained some composure. "But I have to go back to my wife now. She's waiting for me."

"Can't come back to my place just for a drink?" She tilted her head again, moved in closer and brushed her hand over my groin area. My cock was pressing against my pants and she bumped it. "Uh oh." She opened her mouth again in a mocking manner. "I missed that."

I looked around the lobby, wondering if anyone could sense the electricity coming off us. Should I tell her my wife was pregnant?

That could have ended it right there. No, I wanted to see how far this would go. "If we do anything it's as friends."

"Of course." Again she used that new tone of hers, the tone of total control. It frightened me, but also made me curious.

"Then just a drink."

"That's all."

I called my wife, told her there were some issues with a report I had turned in and left with Jenny. We headed straight for her place. When we entered everything was as it should have been. As if I had never left. It was something I hated about leaving for deployments, experiencing so much and coming back to see it really didn't matter. Joe. If only it mattered.

"What have you been up to?" I asked her, as I took her hand in mine. She smiled, knowingly.

"Not much. Same old job. Tried to find a replacement for you." She tossed her head back. "But to no avail. You are irreplaceable." She stepped close to me and we kissed.

I felt great, my blood flowed hard and fast through my body, and I rested my hands on her hips, dragged them down to her thighs, then back up her skirt. Her skin was soft, and through that perfume of hers, I could smell her sweat, and that familiar sex.

There wasn't much to hold me back. I turned her around and she let me enter her from behind, both of us standing next to her front door, which I was certain was unlocked. Within a few thrusts I knew I wouldn't last, I shuffled through the possibilities of changing positions, thinking of something else to delay the inevitable climax. No, there was no need; I wanted to enjoy the moment for what it was. I looked over her hiked up skirt, tensed legs, turned face with that cute nose and I shriveled over like a man shot.

"Oh, yeah," she said, uncharacteristically, but I decided not to worry about what changes had come to her. Perhaps she was finally opening up, perhaps she had learned to say things that made men smile, or perhaps she had a previous man who told her what to say.

"Damn," I said and walked her to her bed. We spent the rest of the day exploring each other. At one point I felt such a happiness sitting amongst her giggles and strokes that I wondered why I would go back to my wife. Then I remembered the sound advice from my military days: never fuck someone better looking than your wife, because then you start thinking about leaving your wife. Had I made that mistake? Jenny was a fine physical specimen of a woman, the best I had seen, and now it seemed that I like other things about her even more. More than my wife? That was a dangerous thought.

But there was something in her that left me helpless. When had I last felt like that with my old lady; when had I *ever* felt like that with her, with anyone?

Jenny brought over a fruit salad from the kitchen. "For my man."

I wasn't certain how to take that, was it sinister? Would she become a stalker? No matter what transpired here, and how I felt, I had a wife with my child further uptown. I wouldn't want that destroyed, would I? Still, her facial expression told me that she didn't mean it beyond some more teasing.

It was then that I noticed that the pain in my arms had been delayed since seeing her in the lobby, and now after holding out for so long it was coming back to life inside me.

I looked at a necklace on her night table. It was had a dollar shell attached to it. Joe had one exactly like it. Wore it one time we had hit up Nags Head in North Carolina trying to find some Southern tail between training sessions.

Poor bastard, I thought, he really didn't deserve to die. Yet, what kind of thought was that? If I really could switch places with him would I? And would that be fair to my wife, my child... Jenny? A cold feeling came over me as I thought of Joe's body, mangled, all started by a group of misfits who claimed to be Taliban, but were really just opium growers who were angry with the government for destroying their crops while allowing the friends of the government to continue growing them.

What a mess.

Everything had been a mess. Iraq had been the same. For all the grandiose talk in both wars shitty squabbles is what it came down to. I thought of our side, the generals I saw, the money exchanged. I wasn't certain what to make of it. Surely they were good? Perhaps I was being too soft about the death of a friend. Better to double down and believe with more fervor, I suppose. But

I wasn't like that. I was glad that I wouldn't be going over any more.

"What's on your mind?" Jenny looked at me when I didn't touch any of her fruit.

"Oh, nothing." I grabbed some mango pieces. "Mmgood," I said and chewed down a few more.

"Come on, you were thinking about something. Was it your secret mission?" Her eyes lightened up when she said that.

My paranoia jumped slightly, but it was lost in my affection for Jenny. "Nothing much." I pondered telling her about Joe. It wouldn't require telling her about the meat of the mission. I had to get this off my chest, or I was liable to burst at an inopportune moment in the subway. Her big eyes were looking at me, her lips bursting below. "Well, you can't tell anyone about this, all right?"

Her eyes widened. "Oh my, Matt, this *is* something secret." She sidled up next to me and took a hold of my hand, my thigh. "I won't tell anyone. I promise."

"I was in Afghanistan, near the border, with a good friend of mine. From the military. He died out there, mortar. Freak attack, really. But I suppose most of them are freakish. Ever since then, more so than before, I have been in this funk, angry, at... Well I don't know what." At the end I had started to mumble, yet I knew that didn't matter, what mattered was that I had said something in the presence of someone, someone I cared about.

"I'm sorry about your friend."

It was a cliché, and I immediately regretted my confession. This wasn't for her. She was just a pretty girl that was meant to be tasted every now and then. What was I thinking? "No, don't be."

"No, I really am. It must feel horrible to go through something like that, then come back here and see every thing has stayed the same." She squeezed my hand.

I held back the urge to get anymore emotional in front of her. We finished the fruit bowl and made love again.

"You should be heading back to your old lady, shouldn't you?"

It was evening and I had just taken a shower, we were sitting on her bed. "Yes," I said rather unconvincingly.

"Or." She ran her finger over my nipple and down to my cock. "You can tell her you have to work all night."

I stared at Jenny's wall that was now sporting a new mirror with a rustic rusting frame. "I can't." I turned to kiss her. Her face didn't betray a single emotion.

"That's fine."

I changed into my clothes as we both took each other in; something had definitely changed in her. I would have loved to find out what or how, but I had neither the time nor the patience for that, I would enjoy whatever time I could spend with her.

"There's a party I want you to come with me to," she said, a sly look coming over her face again.

"Sure, when is it?"

"Tomorrow."

I paused, I wasn't certain if I had plans with the old lady, but I could ditch them for another look at Jenny. I stretched out my arms. The pain lingered, but was getting dull, even hinted at strengthening themselves. "I'll email you, all right?"

*

The wife seemed to brood when I told her I had more work the next day. We fought about money, but when I promised to take a few days off from work, she agreed. I felt bad, but only for the moments when I looked at her. I loved her, and hoped that she would never think badly of me. I tried not to act so giddy when I left, and I promised to be back as soon as the work was over. I put on a pair of brown wingtips, dress jeans, and a blue sport jacket and gave her a kiss as I left. I was wearing the cologne she had bought for me for our anniversary.

At the 205th station, waiting for the D-train, I noticed the same homeless man I had paid the other day sitting on a bench. My arms definitely remembered and a sharp pain went through them. I pulled up my traps and shook out my hands. In the corner of my eye I could feel the man staring at me. So many homeless in the City. I had always thought that they were merely there for scam of getting people's money. I only ever gave to entertainers on the subway.

The writer in me told me to go over and talk. I stepped over to him. There was something about his face, his height, six foot, and build that told me he could have been more than just some homeless man.

"Spiderman." He smiled as I walked up to him.

"How are you?" I put out my hand.

"Very well, thank you. I haven't eaten this well in ages. Thanks for the money."

"Thanks for your help." I grinned. His aura, his energy, was obvious. This man could easily have led people to the chosen land. Instead he was here, fighting for scraps. Perhaps a thousand year ago and he would have had his own religion named after him. "Your name?"

"Smellgood." He shook my hand, "and I guess you don't give out your name."

His demeanor, everything was wrapped in class, a time in his life when someone told him to act properly, to behave properly.

"Why wouldn't I?" I said, trying to act surprised, but very aware of the intelligence behind his statement.

He cocked his head and raised his eyebrows. "Come on, now. You and I both know that there ain't no place for sentimentality in your line of work. You're a hard motherfucka, and I'm cool with that."

"Matt," I said, more to surprise him than anything else.

His reaction seemed to speak of disappointed man, in what I had just done, in humanity. I sensed that he was perhaps the kind of man who appreciated loyalty to a creed more than anything else. That just didn't seem like the right attitude for a homeless man to have, a man who seemed to have thrown off all shackles of social well-being and loyalty.

And with that I was hit with a memory of Joe, his laugh, his loyalty. Stronger than mine until the end. And for what? I had told Joe before he died that I felt I was skipping out, that I was tired of the line of work, but that hadn't been the entire truth, because behind it all there was something more than that, there was the gnawing need to... I don't know.

"So how'd you end up here, doing this?" I asked. Again I looked him over, standing there in the middle of the platform, his duffle bag of clothes and assorted items sitting next to him. I realized then that he was not accompanied by his usual smell of dirt, and stewed grim. Perhaps I had afforded him a bath.

"How did I end up here?" he said to himself, as if the question had never occurred to him. "Perhaps I should ask you that. How did someone so well put together as yourself, smart and all, end up jumping out of high-rises?" He flashed another grin, his teeth still grimy as ever.

"You first."

His face formed a half-grimace, he looked me up and down. "All right. I used to work at a bakery here in the Bronx. Best damn pastry maker there was. One day, on the subway I saw a homeless man. Not a normal one, but one who seemed to know what he wanted in life and was just pleased with what he had. I talked to him, and at first he didn't say nothin'. Then when he spoke it came out that he was once a preacher. Knew the Bible. Hell knew every holy book by heart. I read a lot, still do." He pulled back the clothes in his duffel bag to reveal a host of ravaged books and NYPL card. "I knew when someone was smart. 'Why'd you stop that?' I asked. Know what he said?"

I shook my head.

"It's all a load of shit. And if someone tells you different, know that they are fools or know how to live without a heart so white..." Smellgood shuffled his feet and lips. "I got it. Pure and simple. And I couldn't do what I did anymore. I sold all my things, gave them to charity, and here I am today. Never been happier. When I want to I go to the library and learn more. What else is life supposed to be about?"

I nodded with my chin and wondered if he was simply crazy. "So you feel apart from society?"

He scoffed. "I'm taking the subway; I use the library. If I wanted to be apart from society I would have left the City. No, here I just know my place. Pure and simple." He glanced at the dirty subway rails as if contemplating some good greater than either of us.

I pointed to his duffle bag. "You not military?"

He shook his head. "I was in for a few years, but I was discharged for medical reasons. You in during the war?"

I didn't like the use of the word war for a few small skirmishes, as much as they affected me, but I didn't argue. "Yep."

"Well, good for you. You joined up to show the country what you could do, didn't you?"

"I did." Why *had* I joined up? A hard question. I had joined up so that I could fight the good fight. And now? I was quitting, all of it. But for what? A rumble in the recesses of my mind yawned.

"Military ain't a bad thing. Not if you want to simply know your place in society. Have it beaten into you. It teaches people to resign themselves to a greater power, doesn't it? Not a bad thing at all," Smellgood said and shook his head.

I couldn't tell if he was mocking the idea of institutionalizing a person or not.

"Needed in today's world, don't you think?"

His head snapped at me and he took me in with the ferocity of a thousand year feud. "Needed, huh? Suppose if you like climbing buildings it is indeed needed." He spat on the subway platform in disgust. "Suppose if we're to beat the Chinese and the Indians we will have to find a way of becoming even more institutionalized. Correct?"

I took in his revulsion to what I had said, without a murmur; a part of me understood it perfectly.

"Don't mind me. It is a good thing. Knowing your place. You know your place?"

It was my turn to look off at the tracks. The train pulled in and I smiled at him. "Who knows?"

Jenny was waiting at her place. I was late, but she didn't seem to care all that much.

"How are you tonight?" She wrapped her arms around me and I felt my heart jump. I'd better not be falling for her, I thought, as I kissed her, felt her lips, the warm wet hints of more. "You smell good," she said as she nuzzled my neck.

"Great." I grinned, then tried to make my face a little more serious.

I was married. I had a child on the way.

Wasn't I supposed to be the one in control? I had her around my finger and now I can barely control my actions around her?

"Come, the party's not until a little bit." She pulled me to her room.

I followed, happy, my mind taking in her curves as if I hadn't seen them before. The part of the brain I couldn't control played with the scary thought that I would never get tired of her.

We walked to the party taking notes of the other people in the village heading out to their own revelry. Jenny clutched my arm, held me tight. Made me feel like nothing could have been better at this time in my life. The night was another lukewarm one, the temperature much too warm for the time of year, but I welcomed it and the open sky it provided.

"I read some of your books," she said as we passed a street vendor selling books. "I liked it."

I kept silent. I hadn't really talked about any of my writing in front of her, nor had I asked. I was surprised that she had taken the time to read my body of work. Did she feel the same as I did for her? So much of me wanted to break down to her right there and then, that I just nodded my head.

When we got to the party, at the top of a building near Washington Square Park, I almost wanted to break off from her so that I could pull myself together. I could feel the tension tying knots with my guts.

We were allowed inside by two very large doormen, who seemed to have a militaristic air about them. The apartment was large, at least forty people were comfortably milling about, and filled with expensive furniture, which were all made to look minimalist, or at least like they belonged in the MOMA. The hardwood floors were adorned with what looked like tightly woven Persian carpets, and the art on the wall seemed to be nothing but color and factures. The view, one I could barely see over the heads of the guests, was wide and unhindered. Whoever's place this was, it was someone rich.

"I've got to go meet some coworkers, you'll be fine alone?" Jenny whispered in my ear, and when I nodded, she pecked me on my lips and walked away.

As I watched her skirt and tights disappear into the crowd, I felt the weight lift from my heart.

What was this? I never felt it with my wife. Not even when we first dated. This was something else. Jenny's smile, when she pecked me and walked away, seemed to be all knowing, perhaps hiding some mischief. Was that the tension I was feeling? It was hard to place what caused it. Perhaps it was the l-word.

I looked around the apartment, buzzing with the energy of people just starting to know each other, the potential of great bonds still in the air. I decided to talk to some people. Funny thing about Joe's death is that I hadn't written since it. Nothing. Not even the idea behind a story, which is how I usually start my novels. Talking would perhaps open up that box again.

"Matt?"

I heard a whiney male voice behind me. I turned and was faced with a young male, fedora hat on, aviator sunglasses on top of them, and rolled up sleeves that showed a mishmash of fading black tattoos on his white skin. I might have met him before, but nothing in my mind could recall who he was or what he did. "Sorry, have we met before?"

"Yeah." He put out his hand. "You're Jenny's boyfriend, right?"

My flinch must have been obvious because he immediately caught himself:

"Or friend. Sorry, not that I've heard anything, just assumed."

"No, of course, it's fine. We're friends." I still couldn't place him, or what he did, though at this point I could assume that I met him in the only other party Jenny took me to. I shook hands with him.

"I'm the writer."

"Ah yes," I lied, still not remembering anything that might have ever occurred between us. "The writer. How's your book?"

"It's good, I got it published."

"Well, that's great." I curled out my lower lip and nodded my head in measured approval. "Congratulations."

"You write as well, don't you?"

"Yes, I do," I said, though I had the feeling that I had never told him that I did in fact write, and that perhaps he heard it from Jenny. Which, if it was the case—as was the reason for the label of boyfriend—meant that Jenny could very well be talking to everyone she knew about me, and my business. This was an easy way for me to get caught by my wife. "Tell me, how close are you to Jenny?"

"We both went to college together at NYU, and after that we decided to stay here."

"And what are you writing for your next book?"

"No time for that, trying to promote this book as much as I can. After that I'll worry about the next book."

I rolled his words around in my head, still wondering if we had talked about his work before, and whether Jenny had been telling him everything. Partially, I wanted to tell Jenny to calm down the talk. Yet I also felt vindicated. She must have felt the same thing as I did. It was the only reason a woman like her would talk to friends in that manner.

"Have you written anything else?" he asked me, taking a swig from a drink in his hand.

"No, I haven't." I paused, still thinking about what Jenny could possibly have told this man. What about Joe? The very thought that she could have betrayed such an open moment of ours made me furious, and I must have emitted some warning in my face or body because the friend in front of me backed off.

"That's cool. You've written before, haven't you?"

I uh-huhed in the positive.

"How do you keep going?"

You keep living, I wanted to say, and you sure as hell don't spend your life going to staid parties such as this one here. "You manage." I looked beyond him, and I saw Smith in distance milling about with a group of what seemed to be Wall Street business types around him. My heart stopped, I swallowed and felt my mouth suddenly dry.

I could smell the purified air of being better than everyone else wafting off Smith and his entourage. As much as I hated this pencil-necked-probably-writing-about-inane-moments-in-the-City-like-they-were-gold-writer in front of me, he was better than those kinds. Then I wondered what Smith would be doing here, and how I could avoid him for the duration of the party.

Why was I being so meek? I remembered what I saw during the surveillance job. An illegal exchange—I was sure of it. Had they finally listened to the tapes? Were they uncertain about my ability to keep quiet?

Jenny walked across my field of vision and seemed to bump Smith. I've seen a hundred handoffs in my day, from drug deals in the City, in Alaska, in California, to information handoffs under surveillance tinged with the training of school. What I just saw was tainted with the latter. Smith had barely moved when he was bumped into, didn't even look up. He was expecting it.

No, you're being a paranoid man again, I thought to myself. You're getting too caught up in this woman, someone who should only ever be a fling, and you're seeing faces in the shadows. Again. Remember, I told myself, you've just come back from a warzone. It's natural to see things like this and be suspicious. Jenny was just some silly City girl. Fuck her and don't think.

"And how is your promotion going?" I managed to ask before the writer headed of elsewhere. He seemed to sense my apathy towards our common passions.

"Good, a few readings here, and there." He smiled, proud of himself. I had no idea why. I had been to a few readings myself. Horrid affairs. The opposite of what writing is supposed to be, was ever meant to be; at these readings the writer became a horrid mutation between a car salesman and artist. The latter never really showing through. Fake laughs, the whole bit. One conversation revolved around the beauty of smells, from a bakery shop. But it sold, I suppose, and it sold better than the smells of something other than a beautiful upper middle class setting.

"What drives you stories?" I said, unable to suppress a smirk that appeared on my face. I hoped he would say something significant, but I was certain that numerous workshops had driven theme from his literature. At another reading I had seen a writer with a powerful book step back from the precipice of saying something because to offend any polity would have been murder. Was the writer in front of me the same?

"You mean a moral..." he said, the word coming off his tongue like a bug he'd swallowed sticking his head out of the window for a taste of freedom, "theme? No, I think if someone wants that they read a Bible, or something like that."

"You religious?"

"No, not at all. But my writing is for people who want to see good writing. Why, do you have themes?"

"Yes, I have a few themes." Was I just trying to hold something over this nimrod? Most of my themes were sacrificing for a greater good, for the man next to you, never caring about the self, an almost Buddhist sense of being, that I had swam through since I had joined the military. And now did I care for any of that shit?

I tried to think of Joe, but my mind went back to the general I observed, the money that changed hands. For some reason I thought that to speak of what I saw would taint the memory of Joe. My mind loosened in its capsule.

Perhaps this boy, man, in front of me was right in staying away from themes. Perhaps they were only for fools.

And just then, because I hadn't kept my eye on the group of business-like people in front of me, I felt the tap on my shoulder. It was Smith. Smith in an ill-fitting suit and hair cut short on the sides.

"Hello Matt." He stuck out his hand in one sharp movement.

The look in his eyes, everything about him was an officer again, and I didn't want to put up with his presence for another moment. In fact my arms started to act up, and I let them hang by my side to take the strain off them. "Hey," I said and watched, through the corner of my eye as the writer slinked away. "How's it going?" His hand was still on my shoulder.

"Well, I'd say. You?"

"Good." I glanced around. No Jenny, and the music seemed to be louder than usual. Before it had been so quiet you could barely hear the snares and traps of some International electronica rising above the din of conversations. Now, however, I had to raise my voice to be heard. I could smell Smith from here. Proud and just washed. I could smell the shower curtain on this fucker. "Did you want something?" I decided not to beat around the bush and have him gone. I knew we left each other on good terms, but that was for work. I didn't want to deal with his regular Army ways at this moment.

"Come on, don't be so stiff." He let out an artificial laugh, like some alien that had decided to decode human actions, and patted me on my back.

There was something hostile about his look, smile—everything—that I hated and wanted to crush. I thought of what Smellgood had said, huddled in his hoodie on the subway platform. Smith represented the epitome of someone trained to be institutionalized. Probably had an American flag over his bed.

I thought of Joe and reminded myself that I was angry without reason. The flag had helped me in a lot of situations.

"My boss wants to meet you. Loved your report, your work. I told you I'd take care of you."

Good news. More money, that was what I needed. Sad to say, but it did buy the groceries. Soon diapers. Again, Smith's actions rubbed me the wrong way. He had said as much earlier, after I handed in my report, and yet this one reeked of bullshit. "Sure thing, when does he want to meet?"

"Now." His face turned serious, I could imagine his small brain going over the training he received in officer school: 'when you give an order be certain about it.' Then he cracked into a smile, his teeth barely showing. I got the feeling that he hated me.

I hesitated, wondered if I should say no and maybe stop working for them all together. No, there wouldn't be any chance of that; I needed the money. Bad.

"Please."

A silly word, but it worked. I agreed; he turned and walked.

We walked out of the apartment and walked into the fire escape and up six flights of stairs. Smith didn't turn his head once, as if he was so confident that I would follow him and not do something to that head of his, that he couldn't be bothered to waste the energy to check his back. The homeless man's words came over me again.

We entered an empty hallway with one door at the far end. The hallway had white textured walls, light fixtures hung from the high ceiling, encased in brown glass that colored the entire hallway in a light better suited for tunnels. The floor was tiled with a pattern that reminded me of Moorish archways. The aroma, stained with Smith's shower curtain musk, was sterile, as if someone had just mopped the floor with expensive organic cleaners. When we got to the door, Smith knocked on it three times. The sound echoed off the walls.

I could hear some furniture moving behind the door, voices murmured.

The door opened with a man about six feet tall, fat around the stomach, and with a tan that spoke of many trips to warmer climes. His hair was balding and slicked back. His suit, gray, was shiny, well fitting and expensive. His eyes, brown, red on the sides, glanced over Smith without a care and settled to parse me with such ferocity I forgot myself and looked away.

"Smith, come in." He held the door for the two of us.

I walked into an office with an amazing view of Midtown and Brooklyn. There was a desk in front of me, and a set of sofas to my side with a bar behind it, and a coffee table in the middle. All around were filled bookshelves, but I had the feeling that the books hadn't been read.

There was no one else in there except for the two of us, and yet I was certain that I heard several voices before Smith knocked. Was I losing my sense of hearing? I had been through enough roadside bombs in my time that it was a possibility.

"And you must be Matt. It's great to meet you." He stuck out his hand.

"Thank you." I shook his hand; he had a firm grip. He shook hands with his palm down, so that he was on top. "And you are?"

"Hamilton. Mr. Hamilton." He flashed a smile to show his grill of white, shiny teeth. It reminded me of a shark. "Please sit down, Matt. Would you like something to drink? A bourbon perhaps?"

I didn't want to drink anything this man had to offer. His tone was too bold for my tastes. I sat down with my back to the bookcase, though I was certain that it wouldn't do me any good. My palms were leaking sweat, and I tried to remember which pocket I kept my knife in. I had grabbed it earlier without worry. "I'm good for now, thanks for asking."

The two of them exchanged a quick look then sat down across from me.

"Can I help you Hamilton?" I decided not to use the Mr. and see how he would react.

He seemed to ponder on it then started. "Well, first I want to thank you for all your hard work."

He really did rub me the wrong way. If this came down to a fight he would win, but only if I didn't get my knife out in time. "Only a day's work." I paused, wondering if a drink *was* what I needed.

"No, it really was above and beyond what I have come to expect," Hamilton said.

"Well, you probably need to find better workers then, don't you?"

Hamilton let out a chortle.

"Listen, you'd better..."

Smith didn't get to finish. Hamilton placed a hand on his knee. "No, Smith, let him talk. He's earned it. Could be that he is right, that we do need better workers. More ones like him."

I tried to read between his words, his facial expressions, but he had a tight mask on. Smart man, I got that much. And I got that he would try and turn me to do his bidding. The funny thing was, needing money, would I have to turn all that much?

"Well, we know all that you went through."

He reached over for a remote on the table and pressed a button. On the screen a video came on of me. Parking the cars, following the target, walking by the target in the elevator. My blood pumped to my head. I was pissed. So the entire thing had been a setup? Or a test? It could be that they were pushing my buttons. But still, I had risked my health, well-being, for a test?

"Are you fucking kidding me? This was some set up?" I leaned forward. I couldn't see behind me, but if there was someone there, I would make them at least lean over to smash the back of my head.

"Easy." Hamilton raised his hand.

"Yeah, watch what you say." Smith pointed a finger at me.

It took all my strength to hold back from snapping the finger back. "Should I?"

"Your shit stinks too," Smith snapped. "All this surveillance and you never once knew you were being tracked. Did you?"

I fell silent. I didn't. Amateur, for certain. "Well, then I'll give your team a tip of my hat."

"We don't fucking need that. Just shut up and listen."

Smith was very near turning this into a fight. I saw Hamilton glance at Smith with a slight look of distaste.

I looked back up on the screen. I was climbing down from the building. The cameras weren't moving. None of them were. There hadn't been a team. They just knew where I had to be and placed cameras there. Or used the many cameras here in the City. I felt a little better knowing that, but decided not to mention it.

Smith followed my eyes. "Yeah, real professional. How many people do you think saw you? And you checked out so much equipment. How many cars again?" He shook his head as if he couldn't believe he had to talk to me.

He was trying to make me small, tenderize me before they pitched whatever it was they had to pitch to me.

"Go fuck yourself, will you?" Smith spun at me, leaning over the table; the veins on his forehead were throbbing. "What the hell does some regular Army puke like you know about this job?"

My eyes zoomed in on Smith, I could see Hamilton watching us both spar. Perhaps he liked to see the minions growl.

"I." Smith pointed at his chest. "Know a hell of a..."

"Smith," Hamilton spoke up again, his voice was strained this time. "Enough. Leave us."

Smith stared at me for a few more seconds. He huffed out of his nose and got up and walked out.

Hamilton leaned back, resting his head on his hands, a little less on edge now that Smith was gone. "Smith can be a pain sometimes. You sure you don't want anything to drink?"

"Sure, tequila on the rocks please."

He smiled. "My favorite drink." And he walked up to the bar and poured two glasses from a smoky and expensive looking bottle of tequila. He threw in the ice after he was done and set both the tumblers on the table and nodded at them.

I knew what it meant and picked one up without hesitation and raised it in the air. "Cheers."

He picked his up. "Cheers."

I took a gulp, as did he. It was an amazingly smooth; the alcohol veiled behind the agave barely tickled my throat. My head opened up and I looked over to the screen that was still playing:

Me walking into my apartment building in the Bronx. They were trying to get me to react. I wouldn't.

"That supposed to mean something?"

He shook his head. "Not at all. Why would it?"

"You're following me to my house. Where my family lives." I paused as I weighed what to say next, how to gauge his reaction. He was no Smith, and just pushing him wouldn't yield me any results. I waited for his reply.

"Well, that would mean something if you weren't listed on a simple search on the Internet, now wouldn't it?" he asked without a hint of malice.

I stared at the camera that focused in on the window of my apartment. There was enough of a sun reflection that nothing showed up. "I want to make sure that I'm perfectly understood here." I glanced over at Hamilton who was feigning interest in the window. "You will never film my place again. Got it?"

He stared at the screen for a few more seconds before he turned to me. "I understand."

I took in a deep breath. He wasn't wearing cologne. I noticed that for the first time. Nor could I smell his sweat. It was like he was some sterile creature. The smell in here was much like the hallway. I could make out cleaners, but nothing else. I didn't like it much. Didn't like how Hamilton was playing with me. I did, however, like how he had dealt with Smith, and I had to respect how he carried himself.

"Fair enough."

"I like you Matt," he said. "You're bold, know what you want, and you say what you mean," he moved his head with a face littered with concentration. "You like whiskey?"

"Whiskey's fine."

He pulled out his cell phone. Texted and smiled at me. Five minutes later a knock sounded on the door.

"Come in," Hamilton said as he switched off the TV screen.

Behind me I heard the cracking of wood. I turned and saw a gorgeous model-skinny girl walk in with a bottle on a platter and two tumblers. Behind her stood three large men, each at least 280 pounds, large backs like highlanders, and six feet tall, with pug noses, black suits and sunglasses on. I really couldn't remember where my knife was. But with three monsters like that I would need a shotgun.

"Whiskey, aged fifty years. Keep it in a safe. Spent half a million on it. Try some." He pointed at the platter as the woman placed it on the table. One of the men pulled out a long sharp knife and cut the small webbing up top. She opened the top and poured a couple fingers in each glass. The room filled up with the aroma of the single malt. I felt nauseous, didn't even like the looks of the bottle, too ritzy.

I knew this was all being done to put me in a certain state of mind. But why? I was just some ex-military man. Plenty more where I came from. I reached over and picked up the tumbler. Raised it. Hamilton did the same.

"What will this one be to?" he asked, his eyes piercing me.

"To grand entrances."

He smiled. "To grand entrances, and grander exits." His eyes grazed over the woman and man a on to the door. They slipped out and we each took a sip.

The whiskey was bold and smooth, but I hated whiskey, and even this expensive kind wasn't about to change my mind, it reminded me of tonguing really old wood. I managed to swig it down before I had to taste it.

"Like it?"

At first I was going to be honest; then I decided that to do so in front of a man who had yet to say anything that he hadn't first measured in his head, would be foolish. "Not too shabby, must have been aged in some plywood."

He chortled and shook his head.

"Thanks, though." I smiled inside, knowing that he had wanted me to be impressed. Money, it went a long way in life, but I only cared for it insomuch as I could use it for basics. Beyond that it seemed foolish. Especially when it was being spent on whiskey like this.

"Of course."

"Now what is it you asked me up here for? I know it wasn't just to show me my apartment, and try to get me drunk. Unless, you're into that kind of thing."

No reaction. I wondered if he had been trained for this kind of thing, to hesitate before saying something. Most people didn't do it naturally.

"You are aware of what you saw and heard, correct?"

"Heard what?"

Hamilton looked at his whiskey and raised it to the light. He didn't seem certain about how to take that. He took another sip and swished the whiskey in his mouth.

"I saw your work, Matt, I liked it, and wanted to talk to you. Perhaps even offer you a better job. Is that all right? Any time you want to leave, please, feel free to do so.

"You're head of security for the company?"

He looked me over. "Maybe."

"So why should I listen to you if you aren't anything?"

"I said maybe to your question. Nothing more. But I do have the ability to give you a raise. All right? What you did will not go unnoticed."

I wondered if I should be nicer. After all, since he was part of a company, he didn't have to pay me anything. I tried to remember the history of the company itself, or its mother company. The security firm I did the previous day's job for was part of the major surge of private companies that rose up in the aftermath of the fallen towers. I had never really thought about it, but now looking at all this luxury in the room, and thinking about how things got done, it seemed rather crass. The entire thing was crass. I shifted in my seat. I was thinking about Joe, and the general, and now the private security firm. Then I thought about a story about a Senator during the initial invasion of Afghanistan. Visited the troops and the only thing he noticed was that the special ops soldiers were using tires on their trucks that weren't the specified ones made in his state. Never mind that the tires were the best ones for the job.

My mind was wandering again; it must have been the whiskey. I tried to focus on the task at hand.

"All right. What's the raise?"

He pulled out a check and handed it to me. Twenty grand. A lot for a man like me. A lot indeed, it could start out in a college fund for my unborn child. I raised my eyebrows. "Thanks." And I felt immediately foolish once I had said it.

"You earned it." He took another sip of his whiskey. "You know much about this company?"

Time to show off. "Sure, you sprouted up after 9-11 and have contracts with DOD and State all over the world. My guess is that all the contracting I've done has been for you in one form or another."

"That's correct. We've turned out to be the best in counter-terrorist operations, and consulting. We have nothing but the best work for us." He pointed at me. "You are a prime example."

I nodded my head. I liked Hamilton; he was now acting like a straightforward businessman. That I could appreciate. "And what is the promotion I'll be receiving? Because I want to make one thing straight, that I want a good-paying job, but I also want to stay home. The wife..."

"Is with child soon. I know." He raised his hand, palm towards me. "We know a lot about you. I don't want you to take it the wrong way, like some big brother kind of thing, but when we look at our employees, and we place so much trust in them, well, then we like to know things about them. After all, you can find out as much as you want about this company online, correct?"

"Correct," I said, rather automatically, for I wasn't exactly certain whether he was speaking the truth or what I needed to hear.

"Good. I'm glad. Do you know who my boss is? The head of all this, the one who makes everything possible?"

I shook my head, a name came to me, some vague billionaire from some magazine. I had looked this up after the job once I had looked up and found out that the general I saw worked closely with the company.

"Well his name is Mr. Krysh. Do call him mister. Please."

"Very well. I will. And?"

"And he'll be here soon. You will be working with an entourage that is very close to him, so he demands nothing but the best be around him. The pay will be a substantial increase from what you have. Ten times more. But the hours are minimal, and though it takes a few years to be truly close to him, you'll be put on the fast track. Mr. Krysh likes patriotic men. Like you. We've talked to some of your commanders in Group, the people you worked with as a contractor, and they all say the same thing. You are a gem. I believe that." He took another sip and made his way to the desk. "And we would love for you to work with us. You will mostly be working with me, but sometimes Mr. Krysh. He will have a few dealings in the Middle East, and he wants you around. How does that sound?"

I felt elated. All the fears and the paranoia that had surrounded me evaporated and my future, my family's future seemed to be on a tangent to a better life. Even better than I imagined.

"You're starting a family. The health care this job offers is one of the best in the world. Your family shan't go wanting for anything."

I nodded, though I took note that when he said 'shan't' and accent penetrated his speech. He had been speaking in an impeccable, slightly crusty New York accent, and just then I heard some thing European, maybe even Russian.

"Sounds good."

"Great. When he comes, stand up. Please. And just be yourself. He will be the judge of whether you get the job.

"And if he says no?"

Hamilton didn't answer; he looked through the desk for something and didn't raise his head.

The door opened and in walked a man with a host of guards around him. A couple were huge men with traps like the three men who came with the whiskey. A couple were still tall, but skinnier, like tier one operators I knew. Their eyes were darting about, looked me over, saw I was not a threat, and scanned the room for anything else. All of them wore black suits with black ties; small wireless ear buds were placed in each ear. *They* were the ones to watch out for.

I stood up and the old man in a blue business suit and white hair came over and shook my hand.

"This is Matt, the guy I was talking to you about," Hamilton said from the desk.

"Matt, Matt. Yes the spiderman. I saw." He giggled.

I could see or feel his energy, brimming. I smiled; I suddenly knew that I wanted to be a part of this entourage. To help this man. So this is how he took over the large piece of pie he had so far attained in life. "Mr. Krysh, it's a pleasure to meet you."

"Please, sit down. I see you've had some of this whiskey. You like it?"

"It was all right. Though I'm not much of a whiskey man myself."

He made a face that mimicked distaste. "Neither am I. Neither am I. More of a wine man my self. Merlots, usually from the sixties. Those are the best. You like wine?"

"I do. More of a Shiraz man myself."

"Nice, Shiraz is good." He nodded and looked me over, approving, and again I felt giddy. Glad to be awash with his praise. It was as if I could feel the power washing off him.

"You play games, Matt?"

"I do." I thought for a second, not certain if he was talking about the ones with pieces or the one with humans.

"What's your favorite game?"

"Chess is good."

"Chess is good. How do you play it?" He signaled towards Hamilton who reached into the desk and pulled out a chess set. He walked over to the coffee table and pulled out the pieces and placed them on the board.

"How do I play it?" I asked, wondering what he was saying. Did he want a high stakes game?

"I prefer Fischer random. It's a less staid game. You ever play it?"

I knew of it. A concept developed by Fischer to get rid of the memorization of opening moves that had started to plague the game in modern times. Grandmasters would memorize lines twenty moves deep, not thinking, or rather going off book only once they had left the line. It led to too much study and not enough of the 'pure' game that Bobby Fischer so loved. The game required a randomization of the first rank, where all the bishops and knights reigned, thus no two games started out the same. I had never tried it; no time like the present. "No, but I'll give it a try."

"Good." Mr. Krysh pointed at the sofa. Please, be seated. I sat down and he did the same. "Five minute game sound good?"

"Sure."

Hamilton was already rolling a dice, and placing the pieces. When he was finished I looked at the board. It wasn't anything like I'd seen before. Where usually there was the beautiful symmetry of the beginning of chess, here the king was on the left hand side, with his rooks on either side, the bishops followed in the center, while the queen was sandwiched between the two knights. I didn't like it. But I didn't say a word. I slammed the timer. I was black. Best to put white on his toes immediately.

Mr. Krysh played without seeming to strain himself. Every time I paused for more than a few seconds, he smiled. The wrinkles on his face, smoothed over by lotion, and skin blotched by years in the sun, his whiteness still simmering with a tan, formed to make a friendly Rorschach and I smiled back. Liked him a lot.

Liked his game too. It was quick. He developed his bishops, his knights and his queen. My development lagged and I decided to move my pawns to deny him any plants on my side. But it was soon a hopeless situation. My pieces were falling over each other, while his were just waiting for the word to crash my gates.

"So what do you think of the whole contracting business? Especially the past few decades?"

I also didn't know what to say. Should I mention my reservations? "Seems like a good thing. There's a demand, a need for it. And thus the supply must be provided." I could see, in my periphery, the four men behind the billionaire moving, they were placing themselves so that they surrounded us. I wondered why. I really liked Mr. Krysh and felt that he felt the same. I told myself to calm down. Hamilton was leaning against the desk, looking on us like he had seen this a million times before.

"But," I continued. "I'm benefiting from it, so it shouldn't be considered a valid opinion."

"Oh I disagree." He moved his pawn up. He was rushing my fragile line of pawns. Once that was gone, my pieces were too tripped up to provide a good defense. Not with four minutes remaining on my clock. "Your opinion is more valid than anyone's. In fact why should someone who doesn't rely on this business for his bread and water be considered to have a valid opinion? That's the problem with this country these days. There are too many people willing to complain, while the people going the real work. People like you and I."

He reached over and touched my king. I wasn't certain what it meant, but I had to move soon. I could play it safe and slowly get strangled, or I could strike out at him, try to go for broke. With the latter choice I might collapse spectacularly, or pull a victory out of my ass.

With a short game like this sometimes a bold move, that would be crushed in a longer game, could be used to psych a person out. I looked for an opening. There had to be something. His pawn rush was directed at my King, but it left his other side open as well. I could push my h-file pawn and gun for his King as well. If I let him take a piece, I could gain the momentum. I pushed my pawn forward.

He nodded with approval. "What do you think of men like me?"

"Billionaires?"

"Yes, powerful men. There is an ominous current flowing through this country today." He shook his head like a general watching a larger opposing army sweep into view. "People are angry, as they should be. And yet instead of working their way out of it, they choose to blame men like me. As if I wasn't like them once." He paused, his finger hovering over the pawn he had started to bum rush me with.

I tried not to tense up. I wanted him to move that pawn, keep at his attack. I could avert him with my attack and take the center. Still his position was superior and I didn't see much more than striking out at him to throw him off his game. Also, I hoped that he wouldn't continue with this long and tired speech. Was it another test? Because though I liked him, I didn't feel that he was the kind of person I would feel sorry for. I thought of Joe, the general. Was me witnessing that general's shady deal the reason he was here?

His hand hovered back over a knight he had in the middle. I needed him to leave it there. "I worked my way up in life. Then the past few years I was told that I'm not wanted in America." He looked over at Hamilton. "You got some of that tequila?"

"Of course sir." Hamilton walked over to the bar.

"You want some?" the billionaire asked me.

"Please."

Half of me wanted to hear him out. For some reason I now felt a little sympathy for him. I also wanted to see him lose on time. He was still ahead of me, and nothing forces you to make mistakes more than lack of time.

Hamilton poured us both the tequila that he had poured earlier on.

"Thank you Hamilton."

"Of course sir," Hamilton returned to his place at the desk.

Mr. Krysh moved his pawn; I held my breath and moved my pawn up again. One more move and I could start my attack.

My opponent moved forward in his seat, shifted like he didn't like what he saw. He was still up on time. "You came to this country to find a better life, I imagine?"

I looked at his finger, again hovering over the knight. "Yes." Again my paranoia opened its eyes because I didn't like that he knew everything about me. I was also thinking why would a billionaire want to know something about a minion like me? I needed the money, I reminded myself.

"And you've found it, have you not? Opportunity, a good job." His hand gestured towards the room. "And would you have ever managed to gain that without people like me?" He moved a pawn to block mine and looked up at me.

I didn't like to be called out, to know that I needed someone else. But it was a matter of pride. I couldn't afford pride, I reminded myself. Unborn child, family. Don't be a teenager about this.

"That's true, Mr. Krysh. It's people like you who created this country." I stopped to think, but not for so long that it would seem out of place. Was he talking about the financial meltdown from a few years ago? "And people forget that sometimes."

"They do," he said, again brimming with energy. "They want things for free, when they should work for them, and they want to blame people like me for their troubles."

I agreed. In the Bronx I ran into many people who fit that bill.

I bit my tongue and tried to focus on the game. With his pawn up he left a perfect place for my knight to rest. He could try to push me away in a few moves, but it would waste momentum on his part and give me a chance to launch the attack I wanted. I moved my knight.

"Nice move," he said and took a sip of the tequila. His finger came over his knight and he moved it quickly, slammed his clock with loud slap, looked up at me and smiled.

I took a sip of tequila and looked at the clock. He was still ahead three minutes to two. With his knight move he had kicked off a two front rush. Dared me to bring my attack. Games like this were too hard to judge. Especially for an amateur like me who couldn't see more than a few moves ahead. I could move blindly now, yet something in my mind told me to wait and see. There wasn't much to his attack. Yet. I pushed towards his King.

"You see, it's great men who are mocked by those who can't and it was only by allowing them to achieve what they wanted did the world come out of the dark ages. Think about Christopher Columbus. The government tried to hold him back. But he finally managed to seek out his dream and with that he found America, ushering in a whole new era of prosperity."

I pulled myself from the game one more time to think about what he said. He couldn't be serious, could he? He seemed like an otherwise intelligent man, was he really bringing in Columbus into this conversation? And as a person that should be held in high esteem? I wanted to correct him, tell him that Columbus had been lucky, because he had only managed to achieve what he did by not knowing much. His voyage was based on a smaller globe. His opponents were right, he was wrong.

My silence must have made Mr. Krysh uncomfortable.

"All these people are doing is biting the hand that feeds them. You understand?" he said.

"I do," I said.

"Good. I hope you're not one of them."

I looked Mr. Krysh over again. He seemed like a nice man, but there was no way a man becomes a billionaire by being nice. His skin was slightly darker than most white people. His fricatives and vowels held vestiges of a European life; I held my tongue.

The guard behind me moved and I was suddenly aware that I was in a precarious position. I wondered if I was playing for my life here. Nothing in the faces of the bodyguards around me gave me any reason to doubt this. I felt a brief spell of fear. I had seen something I shouldn't have with regards to that general. But surely they knew I would never say anything?

I focused back on the game. I was down to a minute. It was time to make a move.

I tried to see some lines. Then out of nowhere I saw what would work. I left my bishop unguarded as a sacrifice and I pushed forward with my attack. When I pressed my clock, I was down to thirty seconds.

He pondered for a few moments before deciding to take my bishop. He still had a couple minutes so I couldn't afford to make any major mistakes.

My other bishop moved to back up my knight.

For the next ten seconds we played without a word, and without hesitation. My other bishop sacrificed itself on his pawn structure, he took it and I came rushing forward. The attack he had was abandoned to defend against mine, and I chased his King across the board, then, very abnormally, across to my side. My time dwindled down to five seconds, I had no chance to think now. I was down on material and if I didn't get something back I would lose soon. He paused for a second, his King safe on the fifth row. Then he launched an attack against me. It was brutal.

I tried to throw a few more things at him; his king was still hemmed in. There was one more chance. I threw a queen at him. Two seconds left. He paused and took it. His king had only two

74

other places to go, I checked him with my remaining knight. Then again. And again. His king could only move back and forth. One second. Check. Check. Check. Check. I pressed the clock to pause.

"Draw." I put out my hand. I wondered if people usually let him win. If so he could be a sore loser.

"Perpetual check," he said glumly. "Well done."

"It was my only option."

"True." He shook my hand. "Well done. Well done."

"Thank you. Good defense against the attack."

He only looked at the chessboard a little longer then finally got up. "You ever play go?"

"Never, what is it?"

"A more strategic game than this. I like it for that reason. It's less direct than this game."

When he mentioned 'this game' he sounded annoyed that he had to stoop to my level with a draw. I kept silent. I had never heard of go, but it sounded a little far-fetched that a game could be more strategic than chess. I got up to shake my legs out. Somewhere out there Jenny was waiting for me. Had she even noticed I was gone?

"Your thoughts on the men who make things happen in this world?" he asked.

"It is the freedom of charging forward that allowed so many great things to happen in this world," I said, though I wasn't certain what exactly I meant.

Mr. Krysh nodded his head. "I like that you're loyal, Matt, a patriot. I saw that in your file. Sorry about your friend. But sacrifices have to be made, don't they?"

"They do," I said, a chill coming over me as the memory of a conversation with Joe passed over me.

"Sorry, didn't mean to bring up a sensitive subject."

"It's all right," my voice cracked.

"Well, I would like for you to work on my team. Do you accept?"

"It would be my honor," I said.

"Good. Hamilton will fill you with the details and a few things to sign. All right?"

I smiled. Happy that I had the job. Mr. Krysh left like a ghost, his presence trailed in the room long after he had left. I signed a few non-disclosure agreements, and when I saw the amount of money I would be making, I couldn't help but grin. This was going to be the start of something great. I could sense it. The billionaire had chosen me. Surely there was something to that, wasn't there?

I shook Hamilton's hand and left for the party.

It was still packed when I walked in. Jenny greeted me at the door.

"Where did you go?" she asked, with a knowing look on her face.

"Nowhere." My grin was still plastered to my face. I looked around the room, but couldn't see Smith.

"Want to go back to my place?" Jenny asked, her hand sliding across my pants.

We left and she brimmed with energy the entire walk back. At her place she attacked me, tore my clothes off. When I pulled out a condom she said: "No, just you tonight."

It was a blissful change, a surprise that shuddered from my tip through my entire being. I tried to hold back, but couldn't. Everything about her was so perfect, her ass, her lips, her insides. It was only when I was exhausted, my member chaffed, and my balls dead, that she rested on top of me, asleep.

As she lay there, I heard a breeze from the window flutter in, anticipated the cold touch of the outside air, and felt a prickle as it licked my skin like a hungry animal swallowing warmth. I shivered, only slightly, and held Jenny tighter. She was a natural aphrodisiac. Even now, with her eyes closed, lips twitching to some far away dreamland, her skin's heat, the hot from her groin against my thigh, the curve of her ass, round, and the greatest part of her body, a borderline and thighs thick beneath it, breasts soft-firm against my chest, I wanted to wake her up, fuck her, have her run her tongue around my tip, come inside her, hear her moans.

With these thoughts my heart panted like a dog in heat, my cock shifted as it blew up. She was different this one, this Jenny, though I still didn't trust her entirely. Her ability to stream her aura right into my cerebrum, or more like my brain stem, was a fearful thing. And even at my age—around three decades on this planet—I knew I hadn't before experienced anything like her—a perfect beauty, perfect face, perfect body, perfect fuck, perfect smile, perfect words, too perfect, one would say. And I still couldn't believe that a man like me, a man who knew about all of life's surprises was, at this moment, experiencing the breeze from the cold outside like twinkles of electricity from that first hit of weed, and thinking that this was the zenith of life, of touch, of having an amazing woman and being inside her and actually thinking of dumping his pregnant wife for this. After all, I had the money now. I could afford it.

As if in anticipation of this feeling, something inside me kicked up the memory of my wife. The bump on her stomach getting bigger. I hadn't told her anything about what happened in Afghanistan, but she had held my hand when I woke up one night, sweating. She did know how I felt, and though she was nothing to Jenny's gorgeousness, my wife was something else: a rock jutting out in the middle of a flat field, a hint at more powerful forces in life. I should be kinder to her next time, I thought, buy her something with the money I'd earned.

I took in Jenny's body, coming down from the elation of its curves, and was hit with a profound anger, almost the same anger as wanting to crush an enemy, and I was oscillated between the desire to punch or fuck her.

Then I thought of the billionaire. I was happy for his approval. I thought of my trip to Afghanistan, the general I saw at the business deal, and my ferocity grew. I moved away from Jenny slowly so as not to disturb her, and went to sleep with my back to her.

The next morning I had a shower and headed back to my wife. She was cold when I greeted her and I wasn't certain why. Thoughts of Jenny pierced my head, but I tried to push them out. My wife needed me to be there for her. My arms had completely recovered at this point and in a burst of energy I swooped in from behind her when she got off her brooding perch. I figured the pregnancy was making her volatile and that I shouldn't worry too much about it.

"Baby, you want to head up to the Dia?" I asked her; she was still staring off into the distance, not giving me any chance to find out what her depression was about. The Dia was a favorite museum of ours upstate. It was a refurbished warehouse that was made to house modern art exhibits that were too big for downtown Manhattan. Our favorite thing to do was wander and kiss and cuddle through the steel curled shapes of Serra.

She looked at me, anger still in her eyes, but when my smile wouldn't fade she said ok.

We took the train from Riverdale and headed north. I spoke to her about the raise and promotion I had received. I told her I would have to leave, but only for a few days. For some reason she seemed saddened by that.

I remembered some of the houses I had seen in Riverdale. When I told her we would be able to afford them now, she seemed to brighten up. It would be a perfect place to raise a child. As I hugged and played with her frayed hair—she hadn't combed it in a couple days—she gave me an odd look.

We danced through the exhibits of the Dia, and afterwards ate at some cute restaurant in the nearby town. After all the passion with Jenny, I remembered that it was my wife who was able to inspire a serenity with life that I could never find elsewhere. I felt guilty for having been so taken by Jenny, and reminded myself to keep the relationship with her on a strictly physical level.

When I had met my old lady, going to college in the City, I had been immediately taken by the shine in her eyes and her smile that relaxed me on cue. We had spent the vast majority of our first few months together visiting museums while I tried to impress her with my knowledge of art. She put up with it and a few months later we were married, matrimonial bliss; me, an immigrant of Seychelles heritage, and she, an immigrant of multi-European heritage. Like all American immigrants we tried hard to forget our ties overseas and focused on living with hotdogs and football.

On the train ride back the old lady slept on my shoulder. I watched as the lights from the stations we passed flew over her face.

*

The night after I went to the Dia with my wife I found myself answering my phone in the middle of the night as I checked up on my Amazon account to see if there were any recent book sales. My sales had been in free fall for a few months now, and I knew that I needed to get another book up. The publisher hadn't told me anything about when I would see my advance for my last book so I wondered if I should e-publish my work and hope the few fans I had in the world would find my work and buy it. Still, I hadn't written anything in some time, and no idea had come through my head in the time since the last deployment.

"Matt?"

"Johnny? What's up?" I asked, whispered because my wife was asleep. Johnny sounded like he was breathing hard from running.

"You get back?"

Had I called him? I forgot to call him. "Yeah, I'm back. Sorry I forgot to call. Things have been busy. How are things with you?"

"Not good man. Not good," he said with a profound sadness that traveled all the way across the land, and hit me in my room.

"What's wrong Johnny?" I said the words and wondered if I was actually going to help him. Would I forsake my wife, and the job I had? Better to tell him now. "I'm gonna go on another job overseas."

As soon as I said it I heard the silence, or rather the crackle of the line, the algorithm or whatever it was that sensed to sound, bits, ones and zeros, that, not hearing anything decided to at least emit a cackle. It hurt, I felt like a horrible friend.

"You said you would call," he said, though I wondered if it was to himself or to me.

"Johnny, listen. What is it? Are you in trouble? Are they coming for you?" I remembered what he said about his rivals out there. He was outnumbered. If he had been stupid enough to confront them they would come after him. Pure and simple.

"No. Not yet. I just thought you would call," he said, though the last words were faded as the line seemed to take a break and cut out to space.

"I'm sorry," I repeated, angry with myself. Though in the end was I really going to help him? He would have helped me get through anything. I knew that much.

"Shit's just so fucked up," he said, again breathing hard.

"Are you in trouble? What the fuck Johnny? Tell me."

"When will you be back?"

"Soon, it's not a long trip."

"You've always been a good friend, Matt. I love you man."

It was not like Johnny to open up like this. He wasn't the reserved kind, but he was definitely not the kind to wear his heart on his sleeve. What did he mean? Was he strung out on drugs? He was never shy about snorting a little cocaine here and there, but he always seemed to have it under control.

"I love you too, Johnny," I said, feeling a lump inside my throat.

I didn't hear anything else. The line faded, cut off. I tried to call back several times that night, but all I heard was that the cell phone was out of reach.

A few days later I found myself headed to Dubai. I was to meet Hamilton there and run a few jobs for him. My place of residence was the Burj Khalifa. Tallest building in the world, and likely to remain that way because there wouldn't be another person or country in the world who would dare to build that excessive of a building. Still, I was jealous. As an American it seemed like we had lost one more thing that we excelled at—hell could only compete against ourselves—during the 20th century.

On the plane, as I played with a packet of peanuts, Johnny's call came back to me. I had emailed him and not received a single reply from him. His words had brought me down immensely. What was it that made him say what he had said? He was in trouble wasn't he? And if so, what kind of friend was I for not trying to find him and help him? Even if I did reach out, how was I to find him? He could have called from a number of places. Joe's mangled body shifted into my thoughts. Would Johnny end up the same way? I tried to forget my friends and focus on what I had to do next.

I was dressed in a black suit-new-wingtips-no-tie-white shirt-outfit. The woman next to me was some Swiss expatriate who worked for an oil firm. She was a typical Northern-European businesswoman; in the sense that she had a firm, stolid exterior that didn't show the world much love; while just beneath was a playful woman who bubbled up in the wake of her fingers waving about her, the shine in her eyes, and the flash of her smile.

I teased her about her outfit, a typical jacket and skirt, dark blue, and I managed to make her laugh. We parted ways at the luggage carousel, and I took a taxi to my hotel. I was to meet Hamilton the next day.

My room had soft sheets, soft carpets, a living room next to the bed, and a large flat screen TV. Typical for a five-star hotel. It smelled almost like a new car. I called my wife on my laptop and talked to her about my trip. Her workload had increased recently, and she was tired of her co-workers. After a while she took off her clothes and I masturbated. Came on the hotel guidebook because nothing else was around.

When I was done we bid each other goodbye. As soon as I ended the call with her I walked downstairs for some food. I was more jet-lagged than hungry, but I wanted to step away from the laptop. I had a strong desire to call Jenny. If I did that, however, I knew that I would feel dirty about doing it right after calling my wife. Sure, I did similar things in the City. There, however, riding through the tunnels of the subway, in one borough and out another, made it seem like a cleansing process, as if it somehow cleared me of any wrong doing.

I ate at an Italian place that had surprisingly authentic food. Still, there was something off about Dubai. It wasn't a real city. Or at least that was my feeling of the place. It was just too glitzy without much else about it. Like a wider-laned Midtown Manhattan without any village to temper it with some heart.

When I went back up to my room I tried to sleep, but since I couldn't I watched Barcelona play against Real Madrid in a match that mixed the best parts of soccer: amazing skill and grace, as well as ferocious tackles and hate.

After switching off the game so I could at least rest for a few moments, I pondered the idea of the Catalans and the Spanish fighting. It didn't make sense, like some old feud between now non-existent families. A baser part of me, perhaps the part that liked Jenny so much, thought differently; it thought that maybe it was the Spanish idea that was archaic, a forced measure that people will only put up with for so long.

Then I tried to figure out what was I doing. This job was for money, but what did that money mean? Security? I wondered why I had this job to begin with. Mr. Krysh may have liked my patriotism, but why? I was no longer in, was I? And I sure as hell wouldn't go back in. Why? I juggled those thoughts: the one of getting paid to be loyal to someone for money that was tied to a nation, with the one of loosening myself from a nation by being loyal to that someone. My mind needed to be reigned in. What was I thinking? Was the affair with Jenny making me lose my sense of reality?

From the mini-fridge I drank a small whiskey bottle, each sip like a punishment, wondering about what I had become recently. I managed not to call Jenny, even though when I checked my email she had written a couple messages to me. The fear that she would leave me for not responding hit me. I finished some more whiskey to fight replying to her. When I checked my email, it was only to see if Johnny had replied. He hadn't. I emptied the bottle before his last call's memory could bother me.

The next day I met Hamilton in the lobby, making sure to wear the prescribed black suit, no tie, white shirt uniform that these parts required. He was dressed in what looked to be the same gray suit as when I first met him. Except now he had large aviator sunglasses resting on his head.

"Sleep well?"

"Hardly," I said, my head pounding. I wasn't used to drinking that much anymore. Probably my liver was done with filtering alcohol.

"Well, I hope you are ready. It will be a busy day," he said and gave me a look that reminded me of my team sergeant from my team days in the military.

"I'll be fine."

We walked to a limo outside and got in. The driver must have worked with Hamilton because he drove without speaking. We arrived at a building that glittered with a new glass shell, though this looked more like a place of work than anything else.

We walked in; Hamilton swiped a card with a guard and signed me in. On the first floor I went about acquiring an ID card. The woman working the machine was Arab, with a headdress on, and she spoke an impeccable English. Her brown eyes mesmerized me and I had to remind myself not to stare. When that was finished, and I was fingerprinted, we took the elevator to the thirteenth floor. We walked into a room with five white men looking like they had a chip on their shoulders, though it evaporated as soon as I looked them in the eye. All of them were in tan cargo pants with tucked in polo shirts of varying color.

"Welcome gentlemen," Hamilton said to them all. "I imagine that everything has gone well for you? Any hangups?"

The men shook their heads. I had the feeling that they hadn't worked with each other that often. There was that awkward pause of not knowing whether to speak, not knowing whether to be bold.

"This is Matt," he introduced me. "He will be the team leader."

The men all glanced over at me, but I could tell that they were as new to this as I was. I was slightly annoyed that Hamilton hadn't told me about being the leader of anything, or what I was the leader of.

"This is Fred," Hamilton introduced the first man. I shook hands with a portly man, no more than five-foot-six, red hair, cut too short for my liking; I smiled. "Fred was with the Marines. Infantry, 03-07, right?"

"That's right," Fred said, in a forced voice that was perhaps too proud.

"This is Brian." Hamilton went over to the next man who was red from a recent influx of sun, had sandy hair, and a jagged face that swooped down to a sharp chin. He was a little above average height, but he seemed to naturally curve his back.

"How's it going?" he said with a strong southern twang. When he spoke his teeth were tinged at the edges with brown.

"Not bad, you?"

"Never been better," he said, also with a forced pride that I did not understand.

"Brian was with the 75th. 02-05, correct?"

As Hamilton introduced the next three men—James, Mark, and Kyle, all ex-marines, or grunts, ones who seemed to be into the same kind of steroids as they were large armed, as tall as Fred, and wore shapely sunglasses on their brown hair—I kept a grim face when shaking their hands, and when all the introductions were done I felt a strong need to jump ship. What mission could Hamilton possibly have for us out here? If it was simple personal security detail I knew I was going to be bored out of my mind.

"You gentlemen stay here, I'll talk to Matt for a second." Hamilton gave me a come here sign with his eyes and we stepped outside. Neither of us said anything as we walked down the hallway and into a room. The room had a desk, a shelf that was empty and a computer.

"This will be your office. All right? There will also be a mobile one, so you can control these guys."

I looked at him, not making any effort to hide my incredulity. "What is our task?" I asked, staying away from the word mission.

"I see you're disappointed."

"Is this another test?" I took in bigger and bigger gulps of air so that I could tame my anger.

"No, it isn't. Trust me."

"This is my team?"

"For now." Hamilton raised his hands in front of his chest as if trying to placate me. "Today's mission will be a simple surveillance mission. Then from there we'll take you away from them."

"These guys, on a surveillance job in Dubai? Did you see them? They're just begging to get back into uniform."

Hamilton let out a laugh. "Well, then it'll be your job to shape them up."

"How long do I have?"

"A few hours," he said, again his eyes focused in on me and started to parse me into little pieces of flesh. "Unless, of course, you're not going to do it?" he said this as he picked up a file on the target we were to 'watch over'. I looked over several different pictures. He seemed to be a familiar face. He was an Arab, fat, slight stubble, or at least with the kind of facial hair that grows in before the day is over, and overdressed for any occasion.

"These guys ever done surveillance before?"

"Yeah, they had a crash course with our company."

I shook my head. Everyone was getting in on the intelligence-gathering wagon. Now that the war seemed to be winding down, people were looking at the next smart bet for defense contracts. And with that rush came the chaff, and with that chaff came me and a bunch of grunts trying to perform corporate espionage.

After I came up with a half plan, I walked back to the room to talk to the team.

"All right, listen up," I said, as I handed out the photos. "Take a good look. A few times and memorize this face." I handed out the file with the information. Then a map with a few markings. "We will get into position in a few minutes. Then we wait," I tried to read their faces to see how they were taking the instructions. I told each one where they were to be, and what they were to do.

"Roger," they said in unison.

I grimaced inside. "No 'rogers', no 'hoo-ahs' or 'hoorahs' got it? Talk like civilians now. Also, I don't care how you do it, but get into a suit, now."

After staring at me, they left the room. The day didn't get better. I tried to direct them to do as I wanted, but in the end I decided that it was best to use them as eyes on. Anything else was too much for them.

The main thrust of the job was to listen in on a meeting the target was to have. It was at a hotel room. We had all the surveillance equipment that we needed. Since I was the only one who could possibly look like the help, I walked into the back of the hotel. Busy, like all back of the houses, I found a uniform and put it on. Pretended to be a housekeeper, and with a housekeeping key, walked into the room.

The target was supposed to have good counter-surveillance equipment, so I got non-transmitting equipment and planted them in the room: one camera over-looked the sofa area around the TV, hidden in a plant, and another audio-only to listen in on anything nearby. I kept that in a garbage can near the sofa.

Later, after the target left the room, along with several bodyguards and the man he met with, a Chinese businessman, I walked in and pulled out the equipment. The entire time I fumed with the thought that this was all beneath me.

"Good job," Hamilton said when I handed him the report and recordings. "Just what I needed."

"Is this going to be all I do here?"

"You don't like it?"

"No, I don't," I said.

Hamilton only smiled and I left without caring to hear his answer.

In my hotel room I checked my inbox for a reply from Johnny. I sent him another email. I could see that Jenny had sent another message. This one had an attachment. This one was a picture of her in sexy lingerie. She knew what pulled me to her. I tried to call my wife, but couldn't reach her.

I fell on my bed and wondered what I was going to do. The strings that attached me home were pulling harder than they ever had before. I even thought about leaving for New York. I remembered, however, that I was going to get twenty-five grand for a week's work. If all I had to do was mindless tasks, then so be it. I tried to forget my anger and drifted to sleep.

The next few days weren't much better. The surveillance was dropped in favor of a security detail, and now we followed some company men to their meetings, and conducted counter-surveillance sweeps of their rooms. Most of the time they met with local princes, businessmen from around the world, US generals and ex-generals. Almost always cash was handed over, contracts signed. I tried not to let it affect me. But I listened. Contracts for Department of Defense contracts that were supposed to be secret were being handed out. I thought about the Senator in Afghanistan. This was the way of the world, wasn't it? Yet somehow seeing this money in security made me feel like I was in the middle of something wrong. And when I thought of that, I thought of Joe, his body mangled.

Afterwards I went to my room, tried to contact Johnny and my wife, but couldn't reach either of them. My wife at least sent emails, but they were short. I put it off to the pregnancy. Finally, I decided to video chat with Jenny. She answered her computer with a huge smile.

"I knew you wouldn't forget me."

"Hey beautiful." I smiled back, feeling the anger inside me dissipate as her cleavage appeared on my screen. She obliged my commands and stripped and played with a dildo. When I came all over the carpet she had me zoom in so she could look at it.

The next day Hamilton called me in my room. "Get some sleep. There'll be a night job."

"Surveillance?"

"No. Just you."

I hung up and again my fears started to rope in all the possibilities for this change in Hamilton's voice. I had mentioned to Jenny that I was going to some big meetings. Had they tapped my computer? It was entirely feasible. Hell, I hadn't even checked my own room for listening devices. I felt anxious and couldn't sleep. I did one hundred pushups and one hundred sit-ups, hoping to tire myself out. That didn't work. What could they do? Maybe sue me. There wouldn't be much left of me after a team of corporate lawyers ran through me. These days it didn't matter who was right and who was wrong.

I thought of Johnny, I had left him out to dry, didn't even lift a finger to help him. And now if I needed help I would be left to fend for myself as well. As soon as I got back I would find out what happened to him. I had to. What else was there to lean on as a human, if not for friendships?

At night I walked into the lobby to see Hamilton with two large Arab men on either side of him. They looked like they could have been part of a rugby team. Big, with a level of skinny that spoke of a dangerous quickness. Each was in the local attire, suits and no ties. Hamilton was still in his usual suit, though it looked like it had just been cleaned. I imagined him walking into a closet with fifty suits, all alike, and shoes all alike too. The thought made me crack a grin.

"Glad to see you've lightened up," Hamilton said when he saw my grin.

"How's it going?"

"Not bad. Ready to come?"

No, I wasn't, but I couldn't very well say that, could I? He didn't introduce me to the two Arab men. He just placed a hand on my back and guided me towards the door. The two men followed from behind. In the reflection of the front door I saw one of the man's jacket fly open as the outside air blew in, and exposed the handle of a gun.

In the hotel driveway a van was waiting for me. In front was a large man at the wheel. One of the two Arab men took a few steps in front of us and opened the sliding door for us. I saw the side of his face; an old scar from his temple to his jaw, smiled in the hotel lights with a ferocity that spooked me. His eyes didn't seem to have much thought behind them—the perfect kind of man for dog work. Was I being too big for my britches? Or was I just like one of these men as well?

It was a one-sided van and I was made to get in the first passenger bench, Hamilton nestling me in, both the Arab men sat behind me.

Alarms were ringing in my head. What had I done? Was it what I had said to Jenny? And if so, why not just fire me?

"You enjoy working with the team?" Hamilton said as the van started to roll out of the hotel's driveway.

"You know how I feel."

"I suppose it goes without saying that all that you've seen and heard during those meetings does not get mentioned elsewhere. Right?"

"I figured nothing I did with you gets mentioned elsewhere," I said, angry at myself for not bringing some sort of weapon. I had a pen, but what good would that do against the men behind me? Besides, I was certain they wouldn't play fair. Probably taze me and watch me squirm with a plastic bag over my head. I tried to keep calm. Maybe it was nothing, but my paranoia overwhelming me again.

"That's correct." A tinge of sadness flew over Hamilton's face.

For a second I wondered if he was disappointed with my attitude, and I felt bad for letting him down, for letting Mr. Krysh down.

"Is something the matter?"

Hamilton looked at the road ahead. Then reached into his jacket. "Good news is that you won't have to work with those five anymore."

I shrugged. "I did the job, didn't I? For future reference you should get people who've done that kind of work before."

"But you can't teach them?" he snapped. "Sorry, you did a good job. Really, you did."

I turned to look behind me and noticed the two men had their eyes focused on me. Their hands were blocked by the seat so I couldn't see what they were holding. I was certain that they were holding something. My heart started to pump blood, my senses heightened. I looked at Hamilton and wondered if I should at least kill him before they got me. Maybe grab his trachea. Would that be possible at all?

"Is something the matter?"

"No." He shook his head. "Why would you think that?"

I paused for a second. Here was the moment of truth. When anyone from tyrannical state police, or any state police really, to mafia hit men—in the end aren't they the same?—come for people, or come to take people away, they try to take the route of least resistance. That route required a soothing voice and reassurances that everything that was happening was routine, nothing to worry about, because the last thing you wanted was someone who was worrying about their life, or their future. And thus these reassurances—if the people saying them are any good—will be the same, said the same way, with the same attitude, as reassurances from someone who really didn't mean any harm, and both kinds of people point to the person asking the questions like they are the ones who are paranoid. That was what was going through my mind as the car rolled into an underground garage.

As the engine idled, Hamilton pulled out a gun. It was so swift I barely thought it was anything. He handed it to me handle first. "Here, this is yours. You might need it."

I looked back at the men. They had guns in their hands as well. The gun, a nine-millimeter, felt like a familiar toy in my hand. I let it hang, tightened my grip and let it hang from my fingers again. I slid the slide back and saw a bullet chambered. I felt comfortable now. The gun felt like an old friend, made me feel like I could face anything in life.

"You listen to any of those meetings?"

"I heard a few things about contracts, but I tried to stay out of it. Better to know less in those situations."

Hamilton nodded his approval again. "There's a meeting with some Chinese businessmen. The same ones you listened in on."

"Oh? What's this for?" I didn't remember seeing any people who fit that description, but it could have been that he meant people who were proxies for the Chinese businessmen.

"The boss wants us to meet with them and see if we can work something out. It might get messy. The Chinese are getting as bad as us about energy." He smiled. "We're meeting with a lower down guy, trying to get him to give us information."

I rubbed the handle of my gun again, thinking about what I was getting myself into. Was this what I signed up for with contracting? Would I be willing to risk my life for what was essentially some rich man's bottom line? I wondered about that. Before, the surveillance was boring, and since I complained I had been given this job. And before that, in Afghanistan, the job was at least helping the war effort. How much further was I going to slip?

"They're here," Hamilton said, looking at a text on his phone. "You two stay in the shadows. Got it?"

The two thick-necked men nodded and we all slid out of the van. I tucked the handgun into my pants, making certain that it was secure. We walked down a hallway and into an open warehouse with thin walls for cubicles surrounding us. Then to the part of the warehouse with a forklift near the front and various goods on palettes. There was a short Chinese man standing with a bodyguard to either side of him. They too were Chinese, though slightly bigger than the man in the middle. They glanced about nervously. We approached them with a steady pace. I was certain that I had never seen these men in my life, but such I had been to so many meetings lately that it was entirely possible that I didn't remember.

The two Arab men were nowhere to be seen. I imagined they were blocking all the exits. I could feel Hamilton stiffen, as if he was getting ready for some trauma.

"Mr. Lee." Hamilton put out his hand.

"Mr. Hamilton," the short man shook his hand. His English was impeccable.

"Shall we go into an office?"

The short man looked around. "Very well. Let's do it."

In the office Hamilton had the man sit on a chair in front of a desk, his minions behind him. I stood behind Hamilton who was seated behind the desk. The room had just the desk, chairs, cement floors, and cinderblock walls. It was as if the room's lack of decorations allowed it to act as something more than just an office, and that possibility made me nervous. Were we going to hurt this man in front of us?

"You know the terms of our agreement. Correct?" Hamilton asked.

"Of course. I want to see the cash first."

"I want to see the information first."

Mr. Lee laughed and said something to his men, who both laughed as well. One was carrying a suitcase and he laid it on the table, opened it and turned it so Hamilton could see. Hamilton pulled out the files and started to take photos with his smartphone.

"No." Mr. Lee put out his hand. His two bodyguards stepped forward, each with a hand in their jacket. I reached for my gun. It would be hard; I didn't know how fast they were, but shooting two in quick succession, especially since I didn't have that much recent training, would be a hard feat. I imagined that the two goons we had were nearby. What was the signal to them? This seemed horribly planned.

"Take it easy." Hamilton put his phone down and reached into the desk draw. He pulled out a large fat brown envelope and handed it to the bodyguard who was nearest to him.

Mr. Lee grabbed the envelope from the guard and undid the fastener. He looked through its innards and pulled out some wads of cash. Dollars. Hundred dollar bills. He pulled a few out at random and held them out to the light. After a few minutes of this he counted the money.

"What is this? There is only half."

"I scan these and you get the rest. I have to make sure this all checks out."

I smiled at the bodyguards who had decided to look at me. I moved my hand slowly from where my gun was placed. The smile felt out of place so I returned to a grim mask. Better have them scared rather than friendly. They glanced around and at their boss.

When Hamilton was done with the scanning he waited for a phone call.

"Checks out? Very well. Thanks." He hung up and called another number. "Send in what we owe them."

The way he said it, the words, the growl in his voice made me wonder if he was going to cap them both right there. A knock came on the door and the two Arab men walked in with another envelope.

Mr. Lee grabbed it, repeated the same ritual before and smiled. "Well it has been great doing business with you."

"Likewise." Hamilton shook his hand. "These gentlemen." He nodded at the two goons, "will lead you out of here."

We watched them as they walked out of the room. Hamilton seemed to follow them, but he only shut the door behind them.

I wasn't expecting him to look at me like that. It was a vile stare, as if he was disgusted with my actions.

"That's it?" I asked, trying to break the silence between us.

He raised his hand to keep me quiet and picked up his phone. "They've left? Good, get the van ready."

He looked at me. "Yes. That's it."

I nodded my head, felt kind of dumb for standing there without something to say. "Good. For the night too?"

"I'll be the judge of that."

The quickness with which he replied, the anger simmering behind his voice, all hit me at the same time, and I felt like a child who was being spanked by his father. Why? "What do you mean?" my voice cracked, was I more scared than I thought?

Hamilton examined me, like he knew he had total control of my destiny.

I took in a deep breath. My stomach rumbled, I could feel my nerves rebelling; my head was being by my skull.

"What just transpired here?"

Was that it? Was he trying to make some point about secrecy? "Nothing."

"Nothing?"

"Uh. Yea, nothing."

He shook his head. "No," he said in a louder voice. "Tell me what just happened."

"What do you mean?"

"You're not stupid, so how could you possibly wonder what it is I mean?" his voice had changed, when he spoke. He positioned himself in front of the door, as if to block my way.

My pride felt punctured. How was I, a team guy, special forces and all, supposed to let some suit talk this way to me? "Listen, Hamilton, if you have something to say go ahead and say it."

"Do you know what I was taking photos of?"

"No, for all I know it was porn pictures."

"Didn't take a single glance?"

I had taken a look, but did he see me look? "Looked, but didn't see anything."

"Is that the truth?"

"Yeah. Listen," I said, raising my voice, because now I was certain. "I'm not here to take shit. I listen, I get the job done with minimal complaints. You want someone else, go to someone else. Got it?"

"You really don't get it, do you?" Hamilton's voice, tight around the edges, seemed to soften when he smiled. "You're in now. Don't try to get out with some cheap copout. Got it?"

Was he trying to scare me? No way I was getting visibly scared, even though inside I knew that he had me wrapped around his finger. Here in an abandoned warehouse, me with a gun that I'd never used, him with more people than I, it wouldn't take much to finish me off and have no one hear of me for the rest of eternity. Tell the truth I hadn't even told the old lady what company I worked for. Or even Johnny. I always wanted to be discrete, now that seemed to be a liability. "Cheap copout? Hamilton, either you make yourself clear or fuck off. If I don't feel welcome, I'll walk away."

"Sure." He curled out his lips and raised his eyebrows to indicate that he didn't care for my idea. "And you'll have every right to. Just answer my question: what did you see here?"

"I told you..."

"Then let me tell you. Because, like I said, you're in. The inner circle. You get that?"

"All right."

"That's what the extra money is for. So I want to make sure that you know what you're doing." Hamilton took a cigarette from his. "You're getting paid enough to know. The information he gave us was for the Chinese plans for the Shenu company. They deal with energy. Know what we'll do with this?"

I shook my head and wondered why on earth he was telling me anything. I felt like closing my ears, like I was a child and he was telling me a scary tale. "No clue."

"We sell it to the highest bidder. Usually the US government, though not always."

I looked at him for a second. That seemed perfectly inline with what the way things worked these days. "So? Is that it?"

Hamilton smiled again. This time his face was relaxed. "Yes, that's it. I said you were in the inner circle, so you now know this kind of thing, but with that comes some responsibility."

"Like not writing about this, or speaking to anyone?" My voice picked up its anger, I no longer felt scared, though something in me told me that I was playing a role. "Is that why you put on this." I pointed at his face. "Front?"

"But you also cannot leave. Or if you do, we'll have to blacklist you from contracting. I know you have a child on the way so the loss of a job in the family would be horrible, correct?"

I paused again. It seemed reasonable. "I have no plans to leave."

"Good."

We rode back to the hotel in silence. All the windows were open for some reason and the chilly winter air buffeted the silence. They dropped me off and I walked to my room. I checked my email, feeling the eyes of Hamilton upon me. No news from Johnny. I had a short email from my wife, but couldn't contact her for a video chat. My finger moved the mouse to call Jenny, then I decided that I didn't need that. Hamilton's actions and words played over and over in my mind. Was he bat-shit-crazy? He had oscillated between anger and kindness, and gave threats like he was a lunatic. I hadn't seen that coming.

I fell on my bed and rolled to my side. I switched on the TV and watched some news about drone strikes in Afghanistan. The pundits weren't really arguing about anything except that the strikes should either be considered a right for the perpetrator, or a violation of rights for the country on the receiving end of them. No one said much about the inherent evilness about them.

The fact that I had just thought of them as such shocked me. When I was working near that same border only a few months ago, I had loved the idea of drones, knew that it would keep us safe. When Joe died, I hoped that a few missiles from the drones would kill the people who had anything to do with the mortar that killed him. Now they seemed like another sign of something that was troubling. Just what I didn't know.

I turned down the TV and thought of Hamilton again. Before all his actions had been measured, perfect. Why would he have changed? There was no reason. His smile during that entire production had been triumphal. What for? I hadn't given any sign of wanting to tell someone about what I did—did I? I felt slightly hurt; I even felt like I had let down Mr. Krysh.

No, but if Hamilton had wanted to say something about a mistake I made, he would have been specific. That had been his personality so far. Or had it? I tried to think of any fault in his previous actions, which would be of any help to me. Nothing came up. There was only the lingering feeling that he had been in total control of himself. If he had been in total control, I had not; I had been unsure of myself and even scared about what might have happened. Did Hamilton sense this?

There were a few more meetings with various businessmen from Sudan, Congo, Brasil, and the UAE. I kept watch over the proceedings. Hamilton seemed as calm and composed as he usually was.

During the last meeting, the man Hamilton talked to was said to have some pull with the political forces in Abu Dhabi. Or so we thought. Nothing Hamilton asked would get a straight answer. He only had one guard, something that should have been our first sign that he was full of shit. In the middle of the conversation that was going nowhere, Hamilton took a call. We were in the same room we had met Mr. Lee in. Hamilton turned to me when he was done with the call and stood up so he could whisper in my ear. "He's full of shit. I just got a call that he isn't who he claims and that he's a nobody." As he spoke I could see bearded man in front of me, dressed in full traditional white Bedouin garb was nervous. "He's wasting our time," Hamilton said. "Let's teach him a lesson."

I pulled out my handgun and pointed it at the guard. "On the floor." I took a step towards him. Hamilton came on the other side of the desk, with his gun drawn. The man smiled, scared. "Please. No harm done, right?"

"The fuck it is." Hamilton stepped up to the man he had been talking to and whipped the pistol at his face. The man collapsed as blood splattered on his headdress. The guard started shaking his head and got down on the floor with his hands rested on his head. I felt bad for him and didn't do anything. Hamilton went to town on the supposed businessman. Kicked him with what I imagine to be very hard-soled shoes, until I finally pulled him away. "Leave him, he learned his lesson."

Hamilton looked at me with a fierce hatred. Something I had not seen outside a combat zone. The guard dragged his boss away after I told him to leave.

I felt that I had finally proven myself.

A few days later I returned to the States. Before I left Hamilton bid me goodbye. "Good job," he said as he shook my hand.

"Thanks," I replied. As he turned I was certain there was a look that bordered on venomous. There was something very calculating about him. I wouldn't be able to say anything about it.

Not for now. Not while I had a child on the way.

Perhaps it would be best to watch him sometime. Everything about what had happened, what I had seen Hamilton do, was beginning to make me feel sick.

*

I flew into JFK and took the LIRR to midtown. There I decided to hit the village just to take a moment to drink a coffee, and get used to the cold weather and bustle that was NYC. But when I saw Jenny not too far away walking on the street and talking to some older woman I ducked into a corner shop. She was still gorgeous, but nothing inside me wanted to see her, let alone touch her, or let her touch me. After she passed by I headed straight for home.

At the 205th station I saw Smellgood sitting on his usual bench.

"Matt." He raised an imaginary glass to me. "Welcome back to my house. Have a seat." He patted the empty part of the bench next to him.

"Sorry, the old lady will be expecting me. Just got back in from out of town," I looked him over. He seemed like he had managed to gain weight. I always thought it was odd to see heavy homeless people, but I suppose there could have been other explanations.

"No problem." He looked at my luggage. "Always gotta please the old lady."

"That's definitely true."

"Something the matter?"

I had been thinking about Hamilton, the steps I would have to take to fend him off, and most importantly, whether anything could be done about him. Hamilton would, should I ever go up against him, have the force of a multinational corporation, and a billionaire behind him. What the hell did I have? "No, not really."

"Still carrying that cross, are you?"

I was certain Smellgood was only speaking in broad strokes and not about something specifically, yet he seemed to have an inkling about my thoughts. "Meaning?"

"When you live in chains you are allowed to get angry at your guard, just remember not to rattle your chains or else you may get punished."

I blinked and stared at him. Was I mad for listening to a random homeless man? A complete loser? The words he spoke made sense for my situation, but wasn't I a madman if I thought they actually applied to my situation. Was I so concerned about Hamilton, so worried, that I had lost control, and was willing to listen to this man? "Thank you Smellgood," I said, and gave him a tip of a hat I didn't have.

"Baby." My wife hugged me, her hands digging into my skin.

"Honey." I kissed her, stroked her cheek, her forehead, rubbed her back. Her presence was such a comfort to me, and all my worries of the past few days melted away as I touched her belly. Soon.

We talked about her work, how she dealt with the pregnancy. Spooning her from behind, I made love to her for the first time in a long time. I didn't last long, but it was a comforting moment, a sexual release that was more about my mind, my heart, than it was about my loins. Afterwards, I licked her clit, my head bumping into the child's cocoon, until her back curled like a tetanus victim.

We lay facing each other and I told her how much money I had made from the trip. She didn't seem too happy about it.

"I'm just glad you're back." She squeezed my hand.

I had always loved her, from the moment I met her, and yet it was only then that I realized that she would always be the only one, only thing, only feeling, that I would ever need in my life.

We watched a movie together and after it was done, she walked up to me with a package.

"This came for you in the mail. The return address sounds bogus though."

I looked at the brown envelope. John Doe. Climax, KY 00069. Sounded like complete bullshit, but who would send me an anonymous package in the mail? I looked for a post stamp and saw that there was only one for the City. That means someone dropped it in a mailbox somewhere here. I felt the inside of the package. It felt like papers and a small CD case.

I opened it and pulled out several papers with handwritten scrawl, as well as a few photos, and hastily drawn maps. It was from Johnny. He had been in the City and not seen me. What a shame. The old lady glanced everything over.

"What is it? A treasure map?" She pointed at a worn out topographical map that had red Xs marked all across it.

I wasn't certain if I was going to be able to read it in front of her. Yet I would be some husband if I were to keep it away from her.

"You remember Johnny?"

"Oh yeah, the friend in the night." She gave me a knowing smile, as if from his demeanor and how little I said to him that she was able to figure out what he did. "You're actually going to tell me the truth about him?"

"What do you mean?" I said, though a smirk appeared on my lips, not because I was caught in a lie, but because my woman was smart enough to figure that out.

"Like I don't know when you're holding something back from me." She acted as if there wasn't a thing in the world she didn't know. "Mister secrecy." Her face turned solemn, as if her words had ignited thoughts and fears that she didn't like. "You shouldn't bear so much yourself. You're only one man. And you should trust me more with what you know. I'm not some child." And with that she turned and walked to her place on the sofa.

I looked at her, heart dropping, like my guts had been ripped out and my heart was slowly sliding down my cavity and would soon rest with my balls. I thought about Jenny. My wife, my everything, and I had betrayed her. For what? A piece of ass? I felt disgusted with myself. Why didn't I trust her with information like this? She could handle it. My mind settled, and the fears and paranoia that kept me alive in more dangerous parts of the world rose up again.

Don't be a fool, you want to drag her down to your level? At least let her stay above you, because that's where she should always be.

"Johnny might have been in trouble the last time I saw him. When you saw him. He was worried about something." I read the scrawled paper:

Sorry about the x's man I had the place marked, then thought people would look on. They're everywhere. I can't stand it. I'm sorry man. But where were you? You didn't call.

Was he on drugs again? Marked the place? For what? I read the first page. It was filled with mistakes and scratches. I had never seen such a mess of the English language:

I miss you. My brother. He's in Alaska right now. wasak, the X is for a place. Once you find it use it to help him. His name is John, I talked about him. A photo. Don't think on me.

Most of what was written between these words was scratched out beyond recognition. Not just a zigzag line through the word, but someone—Johnny?—had taken a pen to the word and turned it into a solid block with scratches in every angle. I looked at an old photo. In it was a young Johnny, barely recognizable, smiling at the camera, his face thin but puffed with baby fat. Next to him was another, younger man, or boy, who was taller, blonder hair, and only shared the smile and nose of Johnny. John, I imagined, because I looked at the other side of the photo and didn't see anything written.

The next page was a passage from a book. I was certain it was copied from a book because it couldn't have been written by Johnny, and the language wasn't what one would use for a book:

but this could not be said of Axel Heyst. He was out of everybody's way, as if he were perched on the highest peak of the Himalayas, and in a sense as conspicuous. Every one in that part of the world knew of him, dwelling on his little island. An island is but the top of a mountain. Axel Heyst, perched on it immovably, was surrounded, instead of the imponderable stormy and transparent ocean of air merging into infinity, by a tepid, shallow sea; a passionless offshoot of the great waters which embrace the continents of this globe. His most frequent visitors were shadows, the shadows of clouds, relieving the monotony of the inanimate, brooding sunshine of the tropics. His nearest neighbor—I am speaking now of things showing some sort of animation—was an indolent volcano which smoked faintly all day with its head just above the northern horizon, and at night leveled at him, from amongst the clear stars, a dull red glow, expanding and collapsing spasmodically like the end of a gigantic cigar puffed at intermittently in the dark.

'Is there no guidance?'

His father was in an unexpectedly soft mood on that night, when the moon swam in a cloudless sky over the begrimed shadows of the town.

'You still believe in something then?' he said in a clear voice, which had been growing feeble of late. 'You believe in flesh and blood perhaps? A full and equable contempt would soon do away with that, too. But since you have not attained it, I advise you to cultivate that form of contempt which is called pity .It is

perhaps the least difficult—always remembering that you, too, if you are anything, are as pitiful as the rest, yet never expecting any pity for yourself'

'What is one to do, then?'

'Look on—make no sound.'

His son buried the silenced destroyer of systems, of hopes, of beliefs. He observed that the death of that bitter contemnor of life did not trouble the flow of life's stream, where men and women go thick as dust, revolving and jostling one another...

Conrad's *Victory*—I recognized it immediately. Though Johnny had hated college and the snarky kids there, he had always been a voracious reader. We had, while dealing weed in Alaska, talked about some of Conrad's work and how the Pole had managed to be prescient about so many things. This passage, two passages actually, were the introduction to the novel, presenting the protagonist in a crepuscular lens, as well as being probably the best string or combination of words in the English language. The second passage was from a latter chapter where the protagonist talks with his dying father; a scene I still pondered over and sifted through for more meaning for the things that matter in life.

"What kind of trouble?"

My wife's words came at me like words from a shell. My mind barely registered it. I looked at the passage. What was he trying to say? I knew Johnny, like me, never had a good relationship with his old man. Or was it something about us? We always had an equal relationship. Though sometimes it seemed, towards the end, I was giving him a helping hand more than the other way around. But that was foolish. It was always a hand across a barrier, not down.

"Baby," my wife spoke louder and broke my spell. "What is it?"

"I don't know. He has two passages from *Victory* here," I shook my head. "Everything else is... doesn't make any sense."

"What kind of trouble?"

As she said it, this time a little tersely, I realized it was the second time she had asked it.

"Bad trouble." I moved my head forward, as if the answer was right between us.

"Oh." She looked down at her feet.

I looked at the small topological map, a USGS mark in a corner. I would be able to match the coordinates with some place in the US, I was sure of that. But all these x's would make it impossible to find. Especially when I looked at the terrain, some of the lines had 3000 feet written in a break between lines and some had 6000 feet written between them. At least I knew it was in the West somewhere.

Another piece of paper had swearwords. Some cursing his luck, Mexicans, me. I felt hurt, but remembered what kind of pressure he was under. Was there anything to give away his location? Nothing, not one thing. Where the fuck would I find him? I looked for an address for his brother. Nothing.

One more page had words that I immediately took for words from the Bible. I'm sure Johnny was aware that he came from a long line of Judeo-Christian people, but he had never been hardcore, or even more than apathetic towards Christianity. Growing up in the West in a high Mormon population area, I knew he hated Mormons, but who didn't? Interspersed within these words were his own words:

Job: My friends scorn me: but mine eye poureth out tears unto God. &. Ezekiel: And ye shall inherit it. &. Ecclesiastes: I know that every man should eat and drink, and enjoy the good of his labor, it is the gift of God.

Doesn't every guy remember every ex of his life?

Corinthians: Let things be done decently and in order. &. Corinthians: But when that which is perfect is come, then that which is in part shall be done away.

Matt, isn't a new understanding the everything speaking to us?

Romans: Who shall separate us from the love of Christ? shall tribulation, or distress, or peril, or sword?

Since everything comes over new decisions I think in terms of God... Never!

Exodus: Thus the lord saved Israel that day out of the hand of the Egyptians; and Israel saw the Egyptians dead upon the sea shore. &. Exodus: And Moses said, This the thing which the lord commandeth, fill an omer of it to be kept for your generations; that they may see the bread wherewith I have fed you in the wilderness, when I brought you forth from the land of Egypt. &. Deuteronomy: And ye returned and wept before the lord; but the lord would not hearken to your voice, nor give ear unto you. &. Joshua: And the lord gave them rest round about, according to all that he sware unto their fathers: and there stood not a man of all their enemies before them; the lord delivered all their enemies into their hand.

Don't ever guess, remember each entertaining sight

Ecclesiastes: Then said I in my heart, as it happeneth to the fool, so it happeneth even to me; and why was I then more wise? Then I said in my heart, that this also is vanity. &. Ecclesiastes: As he came forth of his mother's womb, naked shall he return to go as he came, and shall take nothing of his labour, which he may carry away in his hand.

Matt, isn't a new understanding that each silly thing idiots believe?

Revelation: And here is the mind which hath wisdom. &. Genesis: And the lord said unto Cain, where is Abel thy brother? And he said, I know not: Am I my brother's keeper? &. Luke: Foras much as many have taken in hand set forth in order a declaration of those things which are most surely believed among us &. Ecclesiastes: For that which befalleth the sons of men befalleth beasts; even one thing befalleth them: as the one dieth, so dieth the other; yea, they have all one breath; so that a man hath no preeminence above a beast: for all is vanity.

So each cry opens new deaths so... What?!

I stared at the words. What the hell was he thinking? He must have been high beyond reasoning. And though I didn't care for the religious aspect of this letter, I hoped that it would give a clue as to what he was thinking, feeling, as he perused through the Bible and perhaps felt a touch that I had always secretly tried to achieve but never came close to.

I settled on the more likely scenario: he was mad. It had been too much that lifestyle for him. Why the hell didn't he choose to be a plumber or something pitiful? This wasn't the road for him.

I stared at the Biblical words again. Was it a joke? They seemed accurate, except for one thing: the Lord's name wasn't capitalized in any of the quotes. Was he being facetious? The Conrad quote, on the other hand, was spot on. Was I being irrational trying to parse the rants of a madman? Yet they seemed to be in line with a world; a world that I had now seen more of, and was more inclined to believe was horrid.

The final piece of paper was another one with his personal language. It was written on the back of a map printed from the

Internet, though this one was of the village and had letters above what I knew to be sites of cafes I frequented.

It's okay. I love you man. but I understand. Stay away. I'm poison, I'm radiation. Nothing you can do. Thanks for all you helped me with. take care of your wife.

I walked to the fridge and pulled out a carton of orange juice. I pulled out the vodka from the fridge and made myself a drink.

"Drinking already?" My wife smiled, but I could sense that her smile was not entirely comfortable with the air created by the comment or the idea that I knew someone who was in so much trouble that I couldn't mention it to her. There was no way to explain it to her, but having something like this between us would most certainly leave our relationship, with the newly acquired trust, in a worse state than before. It went without saying, for even after all the other women, I knew how bad it was to keep something secret, especially something she was poking around for.

"Yeah baby. Sorry, it's a weird set of letters. I don't know if he was fucking with me, out of his mind, or actually trying to say something, something..."

"Something worth reading?"

"Maybe."

She got up and came over. I made no effort to stop her though my mind was telling me to make sure that she was never brought into this. She read some of the papers.

"Was he religious?"

"Not really."

"Maybe he found God...You know his brother?"

"No, though he talked about him every now and then. Mostly he was glad that his brother was more straight-laced than he was.

"Some good sayings here."

"I know. But what was he trying to say?"

"They make it sound like he was lost and looking for an answer," I said then decided to remain silent because it didn't seem right that I should involve her. I was actually thinking about Joe. A man who had been religious, not a fanatic, but a man who could read passages from the Bible verbatim, and a man who could dream of the better side of mankind and match it with what he claimed to see.

"No, honey, these passages don't have much coherence," my wife said. "None at all."

I looked her over, this light in my life. She was smarter than I could ever be, but how could she read that and not think that it surmounted to anything? I grew angry with her, wondered how she could be so snooty at such a time. Why hadn't she even bothered to take a moment to consider what the story behind Johnny was and thus make more sense out of those words? Was it part of her upbringing to see working class people like Johnny as beneath her understanding?

Then I wondered about my problem was. Was I really going to dig into my wife for offering an objective view? Just a few moments ago I *had* seen Johnny's words as possibly mad. Was there something else in my reaction? Was she belittling the words of a friend? Was that it?

And there, hating my wife for something so silly, I thought about Jenny. How her firm ass slapped off my thighs, a sound for the passion we shared for mutual exploration. My cock arose, and I immediately tried to control it, to think of the task as hand.

"They mean something."

"Maybe." She stared at them with even more diligence, but I felt it was a show. "I think he might have been looking for answers. But he didn't know what. I suppose anyone who looks for answers in the Bible is looking for trouble."

My hand caressed her arm; she was, at the end of the day, an amazing woman. How could I even think of Jenny? "Maybe he was already in deep trouble," I said, though when my voice trembled it surprised me.

She looked at me, touched my hand with her forefinger, before returning her attention to the letters or papers or ramblings. Ever since I knew her she always loved solving things. "Perhaps you should talk to his brother," she said as she waved the photo in the air.

"I don't know him," I said, wondering if I should talk to him. "Don't even know where he lives."

"Alaska," she said, with the certainty of a teenager; she pointed at the page that said that.

"Baby. Alaska's a big place. How would I ever find him there?"

"Where was the photo taken?"

I shrugged. "How am I to know?"

"Is it someplace in Alaska?"

"Could be, can't really know. Can I?" The questions from my wife were wearing into me. All I wanted to do was drink and ponder. She's helping you; let her help you. Idiot. She still helps you after all you've done to her and you are ungrateful. "Besides, I have no clue if he really wants me to go there."

"I'm surprised he knows how to quote from Conrad."

Again, I wondered if she said that in a good way, or in a way that showed how little she thought of Johnny and his ilk. With that, I remembered to hate a lot of things about the City and all the people who lived in it and thought they were better than people who didn't. "Yeah, we used to talk about it a lot in Alaska.

She was examining the photo again. "What do you think happened to him that would make him send all this?"

That was the million dollar question. Should I have told her my theories? "I'm not certain," I said and stopped to think over the situation. As I did, I knew the longer I held back the more I was going to regret it. "He might have felt his life was in danger. That's the most I can think."

"Legitimately? Because this looks like a classic case of psychosis."

I pursed my lips and nodded.

"Sad, he seems so happy here. What is it in life that ends up driving us to such ends? Desperation," she said the last word as if to herself and I wondered if she could sense that I was holding back, or if she could tell that I had withheld such things as the details of my work, or the other women I had fucked, from her.

Her question, about what it was in life that drove us to such desperation, seemed like the question, that if I found the answer, I would have all the weight in the world lifted off my shoulders. "I don't know," I said, feeling distraught. Feeling like the bad things that had happened in my life had happened for a reason. That the reason could very well have been me, the way I had treated everything. Everyone.

"What's 'wasak'?" she asked, handing the photo to me.

"Don't know," I said, mindlessly as I was again thinking about Jenny, not with a rush of blood to my head and cock, but with deep regret.

"No?"

I took a drink of the screwdriver I'd made. "Maybe it was psychosis."

"But the quotes are accurate, right?"

"Very, but everything that's from him is incoherent."

"Isn't 'ak' the abbreviation for Alaska?"

I looked at her. Her shirt, long flowing, that she wore with her underwear, suddenly looked especially enticing to me. AK was the state abbreviation for Alaska. "Yes." But what did that help?

Then it hit me, hard, like the air in the room had been sucked out by some explosion. "Wasilla. Wasilla Alaska."

"Is that a town in Alaska?"

"It is," I remembered out loud. Johnny and I had been there a few times. It was a small town north of Anchorage. The Wasilla valley, greener than a jungle in the summer with the smell of the local soil's fecundity in the air, was known for harvesting some of the best weed in the world. We had gone there several times to talk to growers and find a good deal on mass quantities of weed, that we then dealt to smaller dealers around the state, usually in resorts, where the workers loved nothing better than to smoke weed and drift their lives away. "We've been there. Just driving through. It's between Anchorage and Denali."

"Maybe that's where his brother, or even he's at." She handed me the photo and went back to her seat.

I sat down and thought. Wasilla. Should I go there? I'd be leaving my wife again, and after the close moments that we had, I was reluctant to tear that with the force of distance.

I drank the screwdriver, smelled the stout vodka as it soothed me, and watched the trains pass before me in my window. It occurred to me that it was sad to watch a twenty-four hour subway in motion. It never stops, no lull, nothing. Just the constant stream of trains going back and forth until, I imagined, the economy of the local area petered out to nothing.

I wondered how many muggings were going on in the City at that moment. Or, in the moments after I figured out that John, Johnny's brother, was in Wasilla, how many men, because it's almost always men, young men, had been driven to such depths of desperation that they were willing to threaten someone with their life for what was always a piddling amount in this decreasingly-reliant-on-cash-economy? How many people, on the other end of that threat, walking down a neighborhood that they assumed they were safe in, felt like their whole world had been upended? What would I have felt if someone ever mugged me? I carried that knife around because of it. Not so much the idea that I didn't want to lose my money and credit card, but rather that I wouldn't put up with some piece of shit getting in over me, in the game of violence, which was still my chosen trade.

I fondled my last thought. It seemed an odd thing to think, let alone say. What was I, a grown man, mainly law-abiding, doing carrying a knife? Wasn't that a definition of craziness? Perhaps my wife sensed that in me. Read what Johnny had written down, *knew* it was the rambling of some nut job, saw that I didn't see that, making me crazy, and now she was sitting in her perch, avoiding me.

As if she felt my thoughts she got up and went to the bathroom. A few minutes later she came out. "I'm going to bed, honey. You going to sleep soon?"

"No. I can't."

"Don't think too much on this. It's not safe to do so." She came over, kissed me. "I love you."

"I love you too."

And she walked away.

After the apartment settled into a quiet snore, I still remained in my seat. My wife's question lingered, or rather it bounced around in my head, or even more accurately it hunted neurons in my brain, shot them in their sleep, and scared the others to action. What did drive us to desperation in our lives? Was my wife talking about us? Is what I did desperate? How about Johnny?

There was no answer. Just a hollow scream. I needed some fresh air. I put on my shoes, jacket, and keys. I left my knife. I would have to be more careful about such things. If a policeman decided to give me a random search and I had a knife on me I would be locked away for a good portion of my child's life.

Outside the warmer than normal air, something that had been happening all too often these days, caressed my skin. I could smell feces in a corner. It was dark, past midnight, and no one was out on the streets. There had been some muggings here recently. What if I was next? So what? Step up and take what's coming to you. You've dodged it for too long.

Again I thought of Joe. A better man than I would ever be. Worked harder, knew more, had a more malleable mind that was able to figure out solutions for an otherwise nightmarish insurgency than I could ever hope. He had died. What did that say? That squirts like me should have been the ones to live? And now Johnny, a man I made a promise to, told him that I'd help him when he needed it, was gone.

I walked past the Williamsbridge Oval. The local playground.

A few months ago there was another mass prayer by the local Muslim immigrants. Not that I cared for what had happened, people can do what they want, but that the reactions from the local, mainly Catholic, Dominicans and Mexicans had been an interesting lesson for any anthropologist out there. I wondered what someone like Johnny would have said. Wouldn't have liked it, I imagine. Whole host of whites out there would be up in arms about something like this. And what about the people who protested the ground zero mosque, would they have been satisfied with the distance from the hallowed grounds.

I spat. Not because of the Muslims, or the protesters, but because of what I would do in such a situation, nothing. That's right. There wasn't a thing I would do. And like the situation with Johnny I would probably emerge vindicated and live longer than anyone who decided to fight.

And where was the honor in that? I had been a fighter in the Army. Hardcore. Loved the dress of red white and blue. Itching to get into firefights, and after a few ambushes, itching for more. Made it through selection, became an even better trained fighter. Then I decided that I had enough of the Army bureaucracy. Couldn't stand it one more minute. It grated against my skin. Made the war seem pointless. So I got out, GI-Bill was great and I cashed in on the living stipend.

And yet the war ground on. Even though I was doing nothing and watching it, hating the fact that it was continuing like some old crazy girlfriend who broke your heart. Like all I had ever done didn't matter. Suppose it was foolish to think that I, a single soldier, could have had any impact on the war.

Back in the civilian world the fact that I had no contact with an ongoing war began to gnaw at me and I soon was itching to get in on some action. Why? Perhaps it was to say that I still helped push the wheels of war forward. To look to the left and right of me and be entirely certain of what I was. Who I was.

So I did the contracting, but each time, I felt it was less and less about an effort and more about me getting money. Who was I fooling? I now accepted the mantle of mercenary.

My path took me down Bainbridge. A police car rolled by, slowing, the cops inside peering at me before rolling on. I didn't know what to think. It was good to have cops around. Yet they couldn't help me. Not in the bigger scheme of things. If I thought Johnny was missing, I sure as hell couldn't have gone to the cops and told them that my drug-dealing friend was possibly missing. Even if I hadn't told them that information they would have run his full name and come up with his history. What that would do? Life was hard for anyone foolish enough to ever cross the line. Or cross the line and not know enough people to protect them, because the idea that there is some line that no one can cross, that no one is higher than the law had never struck me as what reality sung to us.

A putrid anger arose in me. What it was from I didn't know. Was I one of those people who was protected now? Hamilton and I hadn't exactly been doing legal activities. Bribes, and lots of them, as well as the beat down. With or without me such things would continue.

The last conversation I had with Joe came back to me. Had he thought me a coward who was turning his back on the national cause? Or was I being a fool to even think of this? After all, if I played this game long enough sooner or later I too would end up mangled.

And for what? I reminded myself that Joe had been hit by mortars not for some insurgency group bent on evil, but a group that was tired of a sickeningly corrupt government that had unjustly left their relatives in jail and offered them hardly any protection from the Taliban.

Joe and I had been trying to get the local government faction to clean up their act. All the while trying to root out the Taliban elements in the villages they controlled. Some good it did. I shook my head. We had supposedly caught the head of the group that had conducted the mortar attack. So fucking what? One Afghan's word against another. And in the end it was ideas that outlived men and guns and hopes and dreams. Ideas that had the ability to twist men's minds to focus on one thing.

Before I left I wanted to say that to Tim. To say that the idea that the Taliban stand for was better than the one we did. Not in the sense that the Taliban's brand of fundamentalism was better than our freedom, but in the sense that they offered a tangible and immediate one of security and law, while we, or we and our Afghani partners offered only the insecurity of corruption. Of course the people were going to choose them. And for all that I was saying, that I should have taken the place of Joe, I knew I was happy I hadn't died in that shithole for anything or anyone there.

And that wasn't the only example of my cowardice. There was the case of Johnny. You didn't call. He had said that a few times, and though I may have tried with all my might to paint him with the brush of a drug addict or someone who played a game he never should have gotten himself into, I was still a friend who had told him something and in the end failed to live up to those words. Was I fooling myself to think that I could have been anything but the man I was? A man who was willing to be a corporate shill just so that his family had a chance at a life that could be considered luxurious?

I looked up and saw the familiar green globe that signified an MTA station that worked twenty-four hours a day. It was the old 205th. I must have walked in a circle and not even known it. I wondered if I should have walked in there. A man in a hood, slightly hunched over, and with a walk that was highlighted with a forced limp, came towards me. He moved quickly and I hesitated for a second, regretting that I didn't have my knife. My heart squeezed and froze. I took a step in his direction and watched as his walked by. His face was forty, with lines formed from a life that had been too hard on him.

My heart started again. I decided to see if Smellgood was there. I looked to see if the attendant was there, he was sleeping on the counter, and I jumped the turnstile. When I got down to the platform Smellgood was laid out on a bench. I would hear nothing from him about rattling of chains.

I sat down on the bench next to him. My mind was tight, like it had been chasing its tail all day. The wall in front of me slowly melted into darkness.

I woke up to some one calling my name.

"Matt?" Smellgood lifted his head from his bench. "Is that you?"

"It is."

"What are you doing down here with the likes of me?"

"Don't know," I said, rubbing my eyes. I adjusted to the light in the abandoned platform. There was another homeless man a few benches away, stretched out, his black feet with white cracks and a stench that resembled rotten food in an Indian sewage.

Smellgood must have seen the look on my face as I tried to adjust to the smell. "He's not one for baths."

"You know him?"

Smellgood laughed. "No."

I swallowed to wet my mouth since I was trying not to breathe through my nose. A quick pull of air through my nasal passage and I realized that perhaps Smellgood did in fact smell good.

He looked me over. "You want something to eat?"

"No thanks," I said, as he reached into his bag and pulled out some cookies in a wrapper. Even though they were enclosed in the wrapper I was certain that I would dry heave if I ate something.

"You're thinking too much again." Smellgood smiled. His teeth dirty, and a pungent aroma swam out of his mouth. "Are you still angry about not being able to rattle your chains?"

I didn't know if I was disgusted or if I was amazed at some of the things he said. A friend had just sent me a package which, at best, pointed to something sinister happening in his brain, at worst, to his demise, and I was here talking to a bum. Like he could give me advice? And yet—since I didn't know what to make of the past few hours, or really the past few days, or really the past few years, or, if I'm to be completely honest, my entire life from start to finish—I wanted to hear from someone, anyone who was willing to make something of it.

"What do you mean by that?" I asked, hoping that he would think the same thing as me. I thought he was talking about a constriction I had felt my entire life and which I hoped to, sooner or later, to escape, but now, here with the sun starting to set on my life, I had just found out that I couldn't. What was I thinking?

"You mean to tell me you don't know what I mean?"

"No, tell me," I pleaded more than asked.

His eyes darted over me then to the rails. I followed them and saw a few rats scurrying about. Two seemed to be playing a game with each other; they scurried in and out of the gaps between the ties and the rails. Another smaller rat watched them then started to run away, except it had a limp leg and it ran in a diagonal direction before it slammed into a rail, bounced off it and kept running in the same diagonal, and bouncing and running. It disappeared into the darkness of the tunnel.

"What are you doing down here Matt, at this time?"

I took the change in direction for the conversation in stride and wondered if he was just another demented bum. "Just thinking."

"Ah, you got into a fight with your old lady, didn't you?" He wagged his finger at me in a pretend-mocking manner. "What'd you do on that business trip of yours?" He let out another laugh, and some food, or object of another kind went flying from his mouth.

I chortled at the thought. My wife and I hadn't really fought, but when she went to sleep we hadn't been on the best of terms either. "No, not that. Me and the old lady are good. Just other things have got me thinking."

"Oh yeah, about what?"

That was the trick, wasn't it? I didn't know what the hell I was worried about. What was this odd feeling that *something* was wrong, about me, about the work I did, had done, my time in the military, the country, the world? Could it even be considered normal?

"Hard to say." I took in some air through my nose and now I couldn't smell anything, in fact I thought there might have been a hint of cologne coming from Smellgood. Was he a bum?

"The best things are usually just that."

"Fair enough." I had hovered on the edge for too long, I might as well speak and throw off the burden. "A good friend of mine..." it was harder than I thought. Didn't want to appear weak. "He sent a package. Odd. Maps that don't mean anything, words that mean even less. Quotes from the Bible, from Conrad." I tried to see if there was a hint of recognition from the bum, but he seemed as still as a stone. "It's hard to make anything of it."

"This was a good friend?"

"I'd say," I said, though I couldn't really say. What the hell constituted a good friend anyhow? There were so many different things to weigh. It wasn't like the only person you could consider a friend was someone you'd been through the trenches with. Nor was it just someone who could be considered loyal in the sense of showing up on time. It was a connection, wasn't it? The knowledge that the person was willing to do anything for you? Johnny was that guy. We hadn't been through war, but we'd been through some shit. Was that the defining trait? There was a Russian saying that a friend was someone you had eaten a pound of salt with. True. True? Perhaps. Johnny and I only sold a little weed in Alaska. That might not have been the entire truth.

Johnny, crazy Johnny, had saved my ass before the military. We had been in Wasilla buying drugs from a coupe of guys who looked like Athabascan Indians. They were jittery, most likely meth-heads. Because that drug had torn apart villages across America, regardless of race. It was my first time really dealing with big shot dealers. Fifty pounds worth of weed. Enough jail time with that kind of weight. I stuttered a couple times and one of them came at me with a sawed off shotgun, the barrel pointed at my neck, his finger on the trigger, touching it.

Who the fuck is this guy?! I don't know you, I don't know you.

His friend became antsy. I don't know him either. Waste him!

I could feel sweat pouring from my armpits; I had the urge to piss.

Shut the fuck up! Johnny had a revolver in each hand. You two fucks calm the fuck down or I'll blow both your red asses to Hell.

The other friend threw his gun down. The one with a shotgun to my neck, stared at me. I don't know him, man.

Put the gun down or else this entire place is blood. See if I give a fuck. The man dropped the shotgun and his stance. The rest of the deal went without a hitch. That had been Johnny. Friends first, self later. And what had I repaid that with? Fuck me.

"A great friend."

"All right. And why did he send you this? Was he getting himself into trouble?"

A rat climbed up to the platform and I watched as it sniffed around the floor, ignoring us as it came a few feet within the bench. Smellgood tore open a wrapper and threw a piece of a cookie at the rat. The rat skittered back a few feet before it slowly sniffed its way to the food. I thought then that perhaps Smellgood's demeanor had changed.

"He had some issues with the law. Lived in a more lawless state of mind. And reality."

"That's not saying much. Most people do."

I didn't answer. Sometimes it seemed like Smellgood had a grasp of the finer points in life, and sometimes it appeared as if he was just reading off quotes and sayings he had memorized from his past. Most people did not live in a lawless reality. It was why society had been set up as it was.

"And what kind of issues were these?" Smellgood asked.

"I think he might have been in danger. The people he was messing with would not put up with him..." I thought of a fact I heard once from a friend here in the City. The most common disguise for undercover cops was as a homeless man. That way they were able to keep eyes on as well as avoid looks. City folk always keep their eyes off the homeless that way you didn't have to give them money, or worse yet, talk to them. I decided not to give away details.

"Danger isn't bad. But he's a grown man, I assume. What problem of yours is it?"

And there, sitting on a bench talking to a bum, I stiffened my body, formed a fist with my hands. Smellgood must have seen it because his eyes glanced down, up, anywhere but me.

What problem of mine was it? It was, and I knew then that talking to anyone about it was only procrastination. No one was going to tell me to do it, but I felt it and knew that I, Matt, had no choice. And I also knew that Smellgood would be a disappointment. He may have surprised me with his large knowledge base, but his last statement made him another one of the crowd. Someone who learned from parroting. Nothing more.

"You don't like what you're hearing. Do you?"

"Everyone's different."

"True. Or is it?"

Another rat climbed down a wall and onto the platform.

I got up. It was time I left. I walked a few steps, past Smellgood, who had moved over towards the platform edge.

"One last question."

"Shoot," Smellgood said, he was leaning precariously over the edge of the platform, staring at his feet. He didn't look up. I wanted to say something, but felt it wouldn't be my place for such a comment. This was his house, afterwards.

"What *did* you mean about the rattling of the chains?"

"You still don't know, do you?"

"It's why people usually ask questions."

He kept his eyes on the third rail, his legs limbering up, as if he was getting ready to jump. "It's the pull of something wrong. You can't see it though. You can only sense it. Something wrong. Something you can't escape. Most people learn to be quiet. Some tend to rattle them. Those are the people who get in trouble. Get finished. And that's the choice." He looked up now. "Wear the chains in silence, or be silenced. Nothing else," he looked at me like I was a complete stranger and went back to his diver's pose on the platform edge.

In a cafe in the village I sat down for a coffee. I had a few hours before my plane left from Newark's airport. The feeling I had accumulated the previous night had been short lived. It wasn't courage, because I was certain courage lasted longer than that. I bought the ticket as soon as I got back from talking to Smellgood. Now in this cafe, watching all the people scurrying about doing their daily shows, I was forced to think, to believe that I could be making a mistake. Was I really doing this for the sake of a dead man, and the hope of saving another one? Here in the bustle of make a buck I felt foolish for thinking about such otherworldly things.

The influx of tight pants walking by helped to steady my thoughts. I saw one walk by with a short skirt above her thick thighs. I sipped my coffee. I liked this place. It was one of the better coffee shops in the City. It had creaking wooden floors and a selection of wines. Its only drawback was that the young rambunctious staff was prejudiced to play their music extremely loud. Suppose I was too old. I liked the aroma though, wood and coffee, and the occasional cologne of perfume of the person nearby.

A woman walked by outside and the stride, the side profile of the nose, the thighs, oh those thighs, pulled at my mind, my cock. Jenny. I thought for a second. I had promised myself that I would stay away. And yet her body called me. I walked outside. The sounds of music switched to the din of cars, workers and students walking by.

Jenny turned the corner. I crossed the street and went after her. I saw her on the next block. I thought about seeing her. Maybe I could at least say hi, and let her know that no feelings had been hurt. I owed her that much, didn't I?

She turned at the next corner and stopped. It appeared like she had seen someone. At first her face seemed shocked, perhaps even dismayed. Then a man in a gray full-length coat stepped up to her. They both smiled like old friends. Or was it something more?

I took a step inside an alcove and from the angle could see the man's face. I felt nauseous; it was Hamilton. I couldn't believe that they knew each other. I walked closer to where they were. It was Hamilton all right. He held her by her arm and smiled, then gave a light slap to her face. She twisted in place, smiling, seemingly enjoying his transgression. My head started to whine. There was a rush of emotions. I could not think of anything but them. Was she his lover? Were they in collusion? The first time I had met Hamilton, it was Smith who led me to him. And yet it was Jenny who invited me to the party. Hadn't I seen a glance between Jenny and Smith?

Fuck. I wanted to bash Hamilton; I took a step towards them but then pulled myself back. She kissed him, but it seemed like a peck. Even though I had sworn myself off her, it made me furious. I wanted to crush them both. Hamilton would have men around him, I warned myself and hung back as he took her arm and walked away.

I followed from a distance. The streets were crowded, and I bumped into a few walkers who were looking at the buildings. Hamilton and Jenny opened a door to what looked like a residence building and disappeared.

I turned around and walked all the way to 34th street Penn Station. I went underground and was still overwhelmed with what I saw. Was she his lover? She had a right to take in anyone she wanted, after all I hadn't been around recently, and we had never really discussed it. And yet even if she was just a friend, seeing how close they acted was as slap to my balls. I felt like a fool, like everything I had been doing was a dance for men like Mr. Krysh.

I took the NJ Transit all the way to the airtran, wondering about how much of a fool I had been. Could it be that there weren't any other choices for me? What other life could I have lived?

When I got off the plane in Anchorage the cold air hit me like a whore's tongue. I walked to the gate as fast as I could. I bundled up in my coat and scarf. My wife had been fine with the idea of me leaving for a few days. Smellgood's words swam through my mind, blood. Now that I had seen Jenny with Hamilton, I felt like his words were gold.

Who knew? Though Smellgood's words seemed insightful, I was filled with thoughts of why I had, since joining the military, ever felt the need to be such a pit bull.

With my luggage only consisting of one bag, I walked outside to make certain that I wasn't being followed.

I doubled back into the airport when I was certain that no one was after me.

At the car rental place, I argued with the woman behind the counter when they said they didn't have a pickup truck like I requested. When I finally got the keys to a pickup with an extended cab, I smiled at the woman and left without cursing like I wanted to.

A few hours later I was in Wasilla. It was a small town in the summer, and even smaller at this late winter hour. I didn't have much to go on. Just a name and a picture. I stopped at a gas station that was on the southern edge of the town.

"Hi." I smiled at the hideous and chubby looking woman behind the counter. She eyed me, one eye getting larger and the other squinted. It looked rather horrifying.

"Sorry to disturb but I was wondering if you knew a man named John, I showed her the picture. John McKenzie?"

She shook her head, without looking at the picture.

The locals wouldn't be kind to strangers. This wasn't the South, but it still had some provincial behavior.

"Could you please help me? I'm a friend of his brother. Johnny. You know him?"

From the way she stared at the counter in front of her, I figured that she knew something but wouldn't tell me.

"All right, I have something of his, and I would like to return it to him." I wrote my name and phone number. "Please, let him know that I'm here and need to see him. Matt, Johnny's friend. He'll know who it is. Tell him it's urgent."

She was silent, but at least she didn't throw the number out.

I walked out and drove around until I found a motel. It was run down, and the lady at the office didn't seem to want to give out any rooms.

"What are you here for?" She shot me a look of hate. She was at least fifty, white, pale, and with a round body, her cheeks already turning into folds.

"Looking for a friend. John McKenzie, you know him?"

She shook her head. She was a better liar than the younger girl at the gas station.

I didn't make an attempt at any more conversation. I got the key to my room and took my bag inside.

Staring at the old, room, with wood panels, a creaky wood floor, and with an aroma like a dead rat, made me feel like going back home to my wife. I could have a warm loving body next to mine. Instead I'm here in a room with a twin-sized bed, a night table, and a metal folding chair. I pulled out some of my toiletries from the bag and brushed my teeth. I remembered that I had just made it known that I wanted to see a known drug dealer, so I wedged the chair between the door and the floor, hoping that it would at least hold off any would be intruder for an extra second. Of course I had no weapon, but that seemed like the least of my worries. I wondered if it was possible that Johnny and his brother were both dead, and that whoever remained, or killed them, wouldn't take kindly to anyone asking about them. My stomach churned at the thought of walking into another trap. I was a fool. No, I reminded myself, this was something you had to do, so that you can at least know you helped a friend.

I pulled out the package Johnny had sent me. It made such little sense. What could he possibly have been trying to say? That he liked Conrad? Was he reminiscing about the days we had talked about the Polish writer? That wouldn't explain the Bible quotes, though. We rarely, if ever, talked about that. I looked them over. I looked at his apology, or the last page he had scrawled. My throat tightened. It couldn't be, could it?

A loud knock came on my door.

"Who is it?"

"Ela, the motel lady."

I rose up and walked to the door. Ela was standing outside, in the freezing cold, in nothing but the same shirt she wore at the office.

"Yes?"

"You comfortable?"

I looked around; it was already dark though it was barely evening. "Yes. Thank you."

"Well." She seemed suddenly bashful. "I was thinking that maybe you'd want to come eat dinner with me. Seeing that you were from out of town, and probably... hungry. There are no stores open this time, during winter. And I figured you wouldn't want to eat no gas station snacks."

I looked her up and down. She was ugly, well everything but her eyes, which were glacial-blue, and now that she was—flirting or being nice, I couldn't quite tell—it scratched some of her surface and exposed a girl inside her that needed some attention. It seemed odd that a woman, of any kind, would be lacking for attention in Alaska. And in winter of all times. The ratio favored the women. Or at least they had the pick of the litter. There was a saying when I used to maraud around these parts: in Alaska you never lose your woman, only your turn. Nevertheless with Ela's rough exterior peeled back I liked what I saw. This was Alaska, and I remembered how most everyone was willing to give you the shirt off their back here. "Sure, where's dinner?"

She gave a come here sign with her head. And I stuffed Johnny's papers in my pockets, made certain I had the keys, and locked the door behind me. We walked back to the office, through a door and up a flight of stairs. The heater was barely working, assuming there was a heater, and I felt the chill as we creaked up the stairs. At the top she opened another door and we walked into a small apartment.

It seemed cozy, with flower curtains opened wide to expose the evergreen forest that seemed ready to engulf the town at a moment's notice. The kitchen was separated from the living and dining room by a counter, on which was an assortment of empty beers and cigarettes. An aroma of cigarettes, weed, and liquor hit me. Past days I would have loved to nestle myself in such a place. Fuck

Ela until she was a clump of flesh, snoring. I smelled warm blankets as well, the kind of smell that made me want to lie down. Even with round Ela.

"Have a seat." She pointed at the dining table, then at the living room. The table was a cookie cutter circular wooden table you see in department stores around the country. The living room had a brown sofa with a sagging middle, burn marks, quilt thrown over it, and a television resting on the floor in front of it.

Since she didn't specify where I should sit I sat down at the dining room table. The chairs, with hard round backs, were uncomfortable. On the table lay an assortment of books. Lots of books. It was refreshing. I was also pleased that Ela wasn't the type of woman who apologized for the state of her abode. The floor was also littered with shoes, underwear, bowls, and chess pieces. She seemed like someone I would have liked to know. "You want me to clear off the table?"

Ela gave me a glance from the kitchen, let out a hoot of a laugh. "Boy, you don't hear that everyday."

I smiled. "I'm sure you don't. Yes or no?"

"Just make enough room for the two of us."

I moved a few books onto the two chairs that I assumed we wouldn't use. Then I checked out the titles. She was not what she seemed. At first, when I had asked for my room, I had sensed that defensiveness that can come from a person who had been beat down from life and was tired of being outsmarted. Now it seemed like she was indeed smart. "You like Bolano?"

"He's all right," she said, from the kitchen. She was opening cupboards and had pulled out a few cans of food.

"This one's a little daunting. I found the moments of brilliance to be worth it though."

She scrutinized a can with a little too much vigor, then glanced at me. "You think it's too long for me, don't you?"

She *was* defensive. I wondered why. She must have brought up plenty of lumberjacks here. What did they think of these books with foreign names? "No," I said, trying to sound as if I didn't care. "It was too long for me. What did you make of it?"

She hesitated for a second before going back to rustling cans. "I highlighted the parts I liked. Everything else was useless. Well the police reports were rough to read. For me, a woman. But it was all pretty good, I'd say. Not good enough for the hype."

I nodded my head. "True." I looked at the highlights she made. It could have been that they were from my book. She had highlighted some of the passages that I liked as well. I looked at her, now pulling pots out of the kitchen. She looked prettier than ever. That blond hair seemed to sparkle and she moved with a grace that most City girls could only dream of.

"Do you need any help?"

She smiled while looking at something on the counter. "No thanks charming. Just make yourself at home."

"Will do." I read some other titles. There were a few from Dostoevsky, and a couple from Kafka. I was impressed. A supremely thick one was Shakespeare.

And *Victory*.

I stared at it. What were the chances that some hick-girl out here in the middle of fucking nowhere would read the same book that Johnny had read? It was entirely possible that Johnny had been through here. All the weed bowls had been full at some point. My breathing got faster, and sweat formed on my hands.

I picked it out and flipped through it. Of course the first paragraph was highlighted, but did it mean anything.

I looked at her. There was nothing sinister about her. If she dealt with the drug dealing underground it was probably so she could score a few ounces here and there. She lit the gas stove and poured some can's contents into the pot. I could smell the stuffed beans of the chili; I was hungry. And nervous.

I flipped on. Plenty of pages were highlighted. Her writing in the margins was anywhere from asinine: "good stuff"; to thought provoking: "here I am in my silkies reading words from a dead man, and feeling my heart beat to his prose. Oh Alaska. Oh Conrad."

Finally I got to the chapter with the information I wanted. My fingers didn't want to flip over the page. I could hear bubbling as the chili sauce filled the air. The sharp smell of chili powder hit my nostrils. I looked up to see her pouring some red dust into the pot.

She poured some pasta into another pot.

"Dinner's almost ready." Our eyes met when she looked up. I refused to look away; her blue orbs seemed to take up the entire room.

It was she who glanced away, and I could see a tinge of red on her skin. My cock shifted, and I bit the inside of my cheek, reminding myself of the moment I had felt at one with my wife.

But she was so far away.

When I flipped the page I could see the highlights. She too had thought the conversation between the father and son was worthy of a highlight. Don't be a fool, I thought, this was the same thing with Jenny and Smith. You saw a glance between them and decided to ignore it. Now you have a link in Alaska between Johnny and someone who had read the same book. This was Alaska—what were the chances?

When my eyes left the page and focused on the kitchen I saw Ela staring at me. It was a stare that held many owners: desire, fondness, and some need for control. I smiled at her. Again she looked back and stirred the pot.

The smell of the pasta now competed with the other smells in the apartment. I wanted to ask her about the book, but I decided to ease the tension.

"You play chess?" My voice had lowered; it was shaking my head. Talking to her only seemed to increase the voice that must have been speaking to both of us, the voice that said go for it.

"I used to play. Was never much good at it."

"You ever play Fischer Random?" I asked.

Her look said enough. No surprise there, I hadn't heard about it until I talked to the billionaire.

The next book I opened was a Bible. I picked it up and browsed through it. There were highlights everywhere, but she had no notes in the margins. "You religious?"

"I believe in God, if that's what you mean. But I don't go to no church," she said defiantly.

I stared at some of the passages. It was Genesis. It seemed like such a simplistic tale. How those men must have sat around, staring at the stars above and thinking of a place on earth and in their minds for themselves—their hopes.

"You?"

She was at the table with a couple of plates of chili on pasta. Some cheddar cheese was melted on top.

"Wow, thanks." I took the plate from her and placed it down.

"Anything to drink?"

"Water's good."

She smiled to herself and came back with a glass of water and a beer for herself.

"Enjoy."

I tilted my head down in thanks and started in on the meal. It might have been because I was tired and hungry from the long plane trip, the thoughts of my work, Johnny, Joe, but I was certain this was the best tasting meal I had had in a long time. I scarfed it down, drinking water only when the chili threatened to burn the roof of my tongue.

"You didn't answer my question."

"Which one?"

"Are you religious?"

I thought for a second. "Not particularly."

"Believe in God?"

"Don't know. Not anymore at least."

"Not anymore?"

I looked at her. I had a need to open up, but why? You fool. Why do you have this weakness, this need to tell women what's on your soul? Random women too. Your wife you keep in the dark about things, to protect her. Now, after seeing how Jenny, Hamilton—the whole lot—played you, you are falling into the same trap. "No. Not anymore. Complicated life. Too many worries and hates to believe completely in some higher power."

She nodded at my statement and slowly finished her plate. I was finished, so I watched her eat. She had an odd way of eating, before every bite she would push a section of food to one side and then once it was separated, she ate it by lowering her face to the plate and scooping it in. I wanted to laugh, but didn't want to hurt her, and I also found it somewhat endearing.

When she finished she looked up at me. "My ex always said that I took too long to eat." She looked down with that statement.

I felt that nothing else needed to be said. I looked her up and down. Looked at the books. I would be a fool if I didn't ask about the book, but it would have to wait. My libido was invading my blood, and soon my mind.

We sat like that for several minutes. In that time I heard not a single thing. It was always odd to leave the City; any other place would inevitably be quieter. Here, in rural Alaska, it felt like I was in a lost tomb. Nothing stirred outside. And it was only a wayward car that brought me back to Ela.

"Do you want to watch a movie?"

"Sure. What do you have?"

She had three DVDs: *Pulp Fiction*, *Snatch*, and *Amelie*. I tapped her elbow when she showed them to me.

"We can watch in my room."

"Sounds good." I hesitated, then told myself that I wouldn't do anything. Just watch with her, be polite, ask your questions and leave her be.

Her bedroom was small, it barely fit a bed and a closet. The rest of it was a pile of clothes, and I imagine there was a floor or cheap carpet underneath that too. The smell here was different than the other rooms, it still reeked with the runoff of life, but here it was mixed with the smell of a woman's panties, sweat on blankets, and perfume. I liked it.

The TV was small and had a small DVD player attached to it.

Ela jumped on the bed and patted the blanket next to her. She pressed the remote and looked at me as if I was another meal for her. I wondered how many men had sat next to her in this bed. I didn't care. I could imagine the winters getting lonely here and the need to have anything next to you. I was surprised there wasn't a dog around.

"You're a quiet one, aren't you?"

"Lots to think about." The movie had started, but she had turned it down so we could talk. Her blue eyes traveled all over my body. I felt the energy of being wanted.

"Oh yes, your friend. What was his name again?"

I felt her face and eyes were telling me something different from her words. This was what it came down to, wasn't it? She could have been testing me to see if I was legitimate, or she could have had more sinister motives. "John McKenzie. You've never heard of him?"

"No." She turned back to the screen. Two men were talking as they walked through the hallway.

I decided that it was a dead end and I might as well find out more about this woman before me. "You own this place?"

She nodded her head and turned to me.

"No husband?"

"No. You've got a wife, don't you?"

"Why? Is it that easy to tell?"

"Yeah. You can tell which men have a woman at home and which men don't."

"How?"

"Can't really explain it. You breath out confidence and apathy."

"Fair enough." I glowed at her words. "You had to have been married once."

"I was. Many years ago. I left high school when I was seventeen for some no-good weed dealer in Washington. Near Tacoma. After that ended disastrously..."

"What happened?"

"He got caught for selling. Tried to lay the blame on me. Asshole. I was eighteen, so I just ran further away. Came all the way through Canada and finally here."

"What did you do?"

"Slept with a lot of guys, worked as a cook in kitchens."

"Nice." I too had worked in kitchens; until I found that selling weed to the cooks was a better way of going about things.

"It was. Loved every minute of it. Then when working in Denali I fell for the owner of a small shack. Our specialty was baked fish. Fell in love. Not the young kind, but the real thing."

Her hand grazed by my thigh and I automatically took it in my hand. It felt calloused and cut up.

128

"We married a few years later. It was bliss." Her eyes fixed onto a spot on the wall. "Or so I thought."

"What happened?"

"What happens with all men. We were making good money, and making plans for a family, a bigger restaurant, and one day I find him in bed with one of the cooks. Young college bitch from California no less. I went to town on both of them."

"With what?"

"A bat, what else? I'm not crazy, a gun would have gotten me lots of jail time."

"You didn't get any jail time?"

"Some, but I knew the local police. It all ended up being glossed over. But Joe, my husband, had already gotten this little whore pregnant. I'm boring you, aren't I?"

"Not at all." I took my other hand and rubbed her knuckles, fingers. "I asked. Go on."

She looked at me and shook her head to some thought bouncing around her head. "You are something. The girl was too. Couldn't blame him really. She was gorgeous... I tried to destroy him during the divorce, though. Managed to get him for everything he was worth. Got the shack. And sold it as soon as everything was settled. He left for a place in California. Not certain what happened to them."

"And you came here."

"No, I traveled for a while. Here, Thailand. Enjoyed myself. Met more men than I would ever care for. I was smart, of course, I kept the money from the divorce in a bank. When I was done I came here. Bought this place and have been making a nice life ever since."

I wanted to ask for dates, for ages, though Ela was on less-lady-like side, she still seemed like she wouldn't take kindly to that. I looked at the screen which had two men shooting into kids in an apartment.

"No men since?"

"Oh my." She laughed. "There have been plenty of men. But men around these parts are just too. Too much. I only keep them for a bit and toss them when I'm done."

"I'm sure that's nice for all."

"No way. You'd be surprised who much all these manly men want to cling on to a woman."

"Never thought about kids?"

"Some. But it's too late for all that now."

She was as old as I had thought. "So you read a lot?"

"A lot. And you? No kids?"

"One on the way."

"Well congratulations daddy." She turned over to come closer to me. The room was dark enough that she actually looked beautiful now.

"Thank you."

"You love your wife?"

It was an odd question, at least when it accompanied the unsaid question in the air. "I do." I remembered seeing my wife after the trip to the UAE, how grateful my heart and soul had been. With her all was right.

"But she isn't enough."

I thought about that. Was she enough? Of course, if I were stuck on a desert island it would be with her and no one else. "She's enough."

She smiled, her teeth reflecting the screens contents. "You lie." Her hand touched my thigh, my cock, which was stiff.

I thought for a second that I would pull away, walk out of the room, I even tried to will myself to do so, but her hands were expert. They slid in my pants and slowly stroked, her thumb rubbing my tip in circles. I sucked in some air, let my hands move over to her shirt, lifted it up, and undid her pants. She pulled them off with one hand, the other still on me.

Was I really going to do this? I was in the middle of nowhere, I had to find a friend and here I was. But I wasn't here for nothing, I reminded myself, I was here to find clues and she, a smart local, would be able to help me. I thought of the wide expanse of nothing that surrounded us. I thought of *Victory*, she would know how to help me.

My hands stroked her large belly; it had folds, creased from the years of neglect, and was soft, almost melted to the touch. Old woman fat was hated by a lot of men, but not me, it was only different, something else to appreciate in life. Her breasts were long and wrinkled, deflated. Her face was firm and, here where I could only see her eyes and teeth, seemed to belong to a much younger woman. Only her crow's feet seemed to indicate to the life she lived. I could almost see the young Ela traveling across the country, using her body to get what she wanted, then finding her husband and beating him with a bat. That part made me want her more.

I half stood up and took off my shirt and my pants.

She ran her hands over my muscles on my shoulders and my stomach. "Oh my, you are something else, aren't you?"

I half-growled and felt for her between her legs. She was wet. I tried to remember if I had condoms. As if she read my mind, she reached over to the side of the bed and pulled out a packet of condoms. Then she moved her head down to my cock, licking it like she was thirsty, then swallowing it whole. She started to jerk her head around, so fast I thought she might hurt herself, but I didn't say anything, instead I bent over at the massive stimulation and tried to pull back from convulsing too soon. I kept a finger in her, and when we fucked, I was constantly surprised by her dexterity.

When she was bent over, I managed to visualize Jenny before me. I still wanted her. But Ela, Ela was something else. When we were done and the bed seemed to have engulfed the entire room, she pulled out a bowl and packed it with a nugget from a plastic bag that was in her pants. She lit and smoked, passed it to me, and I puffed a few times before I coughed my lungs out. She giggled.

"Not used to it?"

"No." The high hit me hard. Tingled me from my cock to my brain. I had forgotten how good the weed out here was.

I pulled her closer and we fucked one more time.

"You are something else," she said.

The screen was now playing the part where a man picks a sword. Another man was trying to scream with a red ball in his mouth.

"Thank you. As are you. I'm sure I see why the men here are so taken by you."

She smiled.

I waited until the movie was finished before I asked her any more questions.

"Where did you get the weed from?"

We were in the kitchen again, and she was making a couple of peanut butter sandwiches.

"Various sources. I grow some too."

"Nice job."

"No, it's only enough during the summer. Right now I buy."

Her voice had gone tense so I decided to back off from the direct questions.

"I was going to mention earlier that I love *Victory*."

"Conrad?"

"Yeah. What made you pick that to read?"

"A friend recommended it."

"Look, I'm looking for my friend, and if I don't find him, I think he's going to get into some big trouble. You said you've never heard of anyone named John McKenzie, or even Johnny?"

She turned and looked at me, handed me a plate with my sandwich. "What kind of trouble?"

"I don't really know. I think that it might have been some competing drug dealers."

"He was a dealer?"

"Yeah. He was."

"John?"

"Johnny. John's his brother."

I took a bite of the sandwich and we both munched in silence. When she was done, Ela took both plates and threw them in the sink.

"You knew them from when?"

"When I was up here. Years ago. Many years. Me and Johnny worked together for a while, and we did a little dealing ourselves. Nothing much, just being young."

"It's Alaska. Nothing is much here."

"When I last saw him I was heading overseas, and he told me to call him before I left."

"And what did you do?"

"I forgot. Even after he said he was in big trouble, I forgot to call him. Or maybe I didn't want to and was looking for an excuse."

"It wasn't your problem," Ela said with a flippant attitude.

Not you, I thought. You seem to have such a good heart. "It was though. He was my friend; I had to help him out. He's done as much for me."

The look on her face told me she didn't believe me. "Maybe it was the trip that softened me up."

"Trip to where?"

"Overseas. Afghanistan. Elsewhere in the Middle East."

"You in the military?"

"Was. This was for contracting."

What had been an initial hit of pride from hearing military, dissipated into something less caring.

"Lost a friend there who was still in. I think that's where my troubles started." Except, as I talked I thought that perhaps there were always troubles. Or if they did start there was no definitive moment. It felt better to blame something traumatic.

Ela's hand caressed my thighs again as she stepped closer to me. "And what kind of troubles for you?"

I chuckled. "Can't really say what they are either."

"Can't or won't."

"Don't know. Just something that started to eat away at my mind. Joe's death. My work. I hated my work on some level. I just didn't, still don't, know."

"The contracting?"

"Yes."

"Well after the military, I suppose that it was less fulfilling."

I nodded, but she didn't know what she was talking about. It was the same thing. The same thing that bothered me about the contracting, bothered me about the military.

"Then Johnny's letter really put a wrench in things."

"He sent a letter?"

I pulled out the papers, bunched up in my pocket. I showed them to her. She read them. Looked up to me with a smile. "That's why you wanted to talk about *Victory* so much."

133

I felt some blood rushing to my cheeks, though I wasn't certain why. "You see why though?"

"I do."

"Those passages are ones I always loved in that book; they meant so much to me. It was like they had the ability to crack into the unsaid things in life. The things we always strive for and never attain; the things that we are never told, that always linger unsaid by our families, teachers, leaders. Those passages are amazing, and he picked them. What was he trying to say?"

"I like those passages too. I don't know what he could be trying to say. Maybe that he felt the same way that you do?"

"And did you see the map?"

"Yes, it looks like it could be from somewhere here. I wouldn't worry about that though."

"Why?"

"He sounds like he just put x's everywhere just to through someone off the scent."

"Then why include it at all? And why explain it if it's to throw someone off the scent?"

She shook her head and looked through another page. "Was he religious?"

"Not that I ever saw."

"These passages don't make any sense."

"But they have to."

"Why?"

I didn't have an answer for that. Because I wanted an answer. I wanted a damn good answer.

"I think his passages don't amount to much. Some seem like they were picked at random. Like he flipped through the Bible and picked a spot." She handed back the papers to me.

We went back to her bed and slept.

The next morning I awoke to hear bacon sparkling on the stove. I walked to the bathroom, a messy small affair, and pissed. Staring at her moldy tile I wondered why I had told her everything, even showed her the map. She could wonder and take them. Then where would I be?

We had eggs and bacon. Enough bacon to clog several arteries.

"You should take this around with you." She pulled out a handgun from her purse and placed it on the table, along with an extra clip. It was a classic 1911. I smiled and played with it for a few seconds.

"Thanks."

"I figured you're chasing a ghost who deals drugs. Might as well be prepared."

When we finished I helped her wash the dishes. That's when I heard the car horn outside. It sounded like several different cars.

Ela looked scared.

I grabbed the gun, tucked it into my pants and put on my coat. I walked out side so see two pickup trucks, each with a couple men inside. There was no one else around.

I recognized John immediately. His face had lost the fat from the picture, but he looked a lot like Johnny, except that he didn't have any kindness in his eyes. None of the other men's stares were friendly. They looked at me like they wanted to kill me. I reminded myself that here in Alaska there were plenty of places to bury a body, and since I was certain they had weapons somewhere on them, I decided to walk slowly. When I got to the pickup truck with John in it, he rolled down his window.

"You lookin' for me?" he growled.

I could see he had a dip in, and was holding something on his lap.

"Yes. You're Johnny's brother correct?"

"Who're you?"

"I'm an old friend of his. Matt. We used to deal out here back in the day."

His hard face softened slightly. "Guy who went to the Army afterwards?"

"That's right." I grinned, but suppressed it as soon as I saw he wouldn't return the favor. "I was wondering if we could talk for a second. Alone." I could see his friend in the passenger seat didn't want to sit around in a parking lot all day. That also suited me since I didn't want him listening in on us.

"Fine, where did you have in mind?"

"My room's fine. It'll just be for a short while."

He spat some dip out on the ground next to me. "No, you can come with us. You got a gun?"

"Of course. You?"

He looked at his friend with a hint of disdain, got out of the truck, pulling the front seat down.

I got in and the truck squealed out. I felt safe in the back. After all, I had a weapon and from back here I could waste them without much of a struggle. Yet I was sure that if they wanted to waste me they would do it from where ever it was they were taking me.

The truck smelled like body odor, tobacco, weed, and some other chemicals that I wasn't familiar with—a hint of chlorine perhaps. There was a rifle in the back and a host of camouflage clothing. They didn't seem like hunters. Could be that they were just rednecks who shot things on the side of the road.

I tried to remember what Johnny had said about his brother. The memory, even the things I thought he said, were vague, mixed in with other things that I wanted to believe, that I had dreamed for, that I might have been told, and that I might have told myself. Odd that the older I got the more my brain became a soup of memories and hopes. Each thread disappearing into another, especially when it concerned other people's words. The only things that stood out, the meat of this soup, were the actions that mattered, me asking my wife to marry me, the nervousness before hand; even with that, however, my thoughts and fears were no longer clear.

I examined the back of John's head. He had shaved the lower part and looked somewhat militaristic. I was certain that Johnny had said something about him going to college, and yet nothing about this man, or the friends he kept, seemed to fit with even one credit hour of higher learning. His friend was big and, though not fat, seemed destined for a sedentary life. His pale skin and freckles made him seem that much more lethargic. His eyes, darting between John and the road, told me that he wasn't as tough as he had seemed in the beginning. His was the type that gained strength from others.

John, calm, staring at the road like some general at his troops, seemed like the leader here.

The truck took a turn onto a dirt road, and I held a handle in the back and the road got rougher and rougher. There were patches of snow here and there, but mostly frozen mud. A few times the truck got stuck and John pushed the four-wheel differential in and we would grind out of it.

Evergreen trees surrounded us, and darkness—the sun hovered just above the horizon even in midday—threatened to crash in.

Just when I thought for certain that they were taking me out to the middle of nowhere, did I find the trees opened up and we came to a clearing with a couple of cabins in the center. Dogs, four German-shepherds were tied all around the perimeter. They barked when they saw the trucks. These were guard dogs, trained to be mean, and not for companionship.

I didn't like the feel of this. As if to concur, my stomach rumbled, and I started to sweat. With a sense of clarity coming over my vision, I touched my gun to make sure it was there. I felt safe, but wondered if it worked, how well it would shoot.

"Go inside Bobby," John said to his friend, who waddled out of the car and into the cabin. "Come up here."

I pushed the seat forward and twisted my way to the front seat. Next to him I saw that there was a handgun in the door compartment. Even though this was rural Alaska, with guns as plentiful as the weed, I was certain that Johnny's stories of his brother, or at least the ones I remember, were not the right ones.

"We'll go a little further. There we can talk."

"Sure," I said as the truck pulled into a tight dirt road, the needles of the evergreens scraping the side of the truck as we bounced up and up the uneven road. We got to another clearing with a frozen lake before us.

John left the truck idling and pulled the parking brake. The others were back at the cabin, and he seemed to have visually relaxed without their presence. My nervousness dissipated and I felt like I could be friends with John like his brother.

"Johnny talked about you a lot," he spoke the words as if he was getting something off his chest. He looked at me and for a moment I thought I could see a child trying to scramble out of the grim look—the mask?—that he was trying to present. "Said you were good people."

I felt honored, almost vindicated, like those words made this entire trip, including the infidelity that I had only a few days ago promised myself off, worth it. "Johnny was a great man." I gulped in some air when I realized that I had used the word 'was'.

John nodded.

"Do you know where he is?"

"No fucking clue." He shook his head.

From the way he said that, I could tell that Johnny hadn't been the easiest older brother to grow up with. Though there was love in his eyes when he mentioned Johnny, there was still a man trying to beat back his shadow, trying to find reparations for all the wrongs that bigger brothers, and siblings, tend to wreak.

"You know what he was into?"

John's look sliced through me, for even a millisecond it scared me. "He visited me and said he was in some deep shit. Said that he might need my help."

John relaxed. "He was. Didn't tell me much. But he was working in California and decided to run up against the Mexicans. Fucking stupid. Those beaners own that fucking state," he said this with a great disgust, and looked off at the trees as if he had lost something great.

"Yeah, that's what I heard. Didn't seem like he was going to back down." At this point I felt that I should hold off on telling John about the package Johnny sent. He may have been his brother, but Johnny would have sent something to his little brother if he had wanted to. He didn't. He only wanted me to steer his brother onto the right path. What that was beyond me. I wasn't even certain how to approach the steering. It wasn't as if I knew John all that well. All we had was Johnny, but from different angles.

"Johnny was never the type to back down."

"That he wasn't."

"Is that what you wanted to talk to me about?"

138

"I hoped that we could find him, maybe help him."

"Not going to find him up here. He has a warrant out for his arrest here."

"He didn't come visit you?"

"No. I visited him down in California. He was living in a motel in Socal. Seemed scared out of his mind."

"When was that?"

"I don't know. A year ago. Told him that was no way to live, that he should come up here. He refused. No way he's ever going to get help from his little brother."

A year ago. That was before his visit to the Bronx. Perhaps he had sobered up since then. Or perhaps he was already in deep shit when I left for Afghanistan, and when we last talked he was almost a dead man.

"You're not going to find him here. Go to California and you'll find him."

"Where exactly?"

"That's the trick. I have no fucking clue."

"You didn't talk to him at all after that?"

"No. Never heard from him again. You?"

"Yeah, I heard from him. He sounded shit scared. Damn awful mess."

"It is. Damn Mexicans. I mean, why is it that they can come into our country and just lay waste to it? Isn't there someone to punish them?"

"Well..."

"Brown fucks. Fucking pisses me off that they're here, taking over like that. There comes a time you have to push back." He pounded on the steering wheel with his fist. He looked at me, my darker skin color obviously going through his mind. "Not you, of course."

"Of course."

"You served. Anyone who served has a right to be here."

"Agreed," I said.

I had to see if I could help him like Johnny said. How was I going to ask him what he was doing? Those two shacks looked like they could have been meth labs. What could I do then? You're here for Johnny, who asked you to watch over his brother. Maybe he wasn't in the drug game.

"I have to ask, John. What are you into?"

"What do you mean?"

"Johnny mentioned once that you were going to college. He always seemed to want the best for you. That's part of the reason I'm here."

John's face went from curious to angry. "To look after me?

"No. To help you. He said to help you."

"Like I need any fucking help," he growled. "Just like Johnny to say some condescending shit like that."

"I think he just wanted..."

"Bull! I know exactly what he was thinking. Do I look like I need help? I'm doing fine. It was him who needed help. That's how he always was, getting himself in trouble then blaming others."

I wanted to ask how trying to help a brother was blaming, but I held the words in my mouth, pushed them back down.

"You ever think of college?"

"I went for a semester. It was worthless. Not for me. Couldn't stand any of the kids there."

"Never going back?"

"Hell no. I'm fine here."

"You selling?"

He was looking at the orange globe that was the sun setting above the trees and hills. His head snapped at me so hard, with such fury in his eyes, that I was certain he would jump across the bench and strangle me.

I raised my hands. "I'm just trying to help, all right? Johnny was my friend and he asked this of me. For all I know he's dead, and I want to help. He said he wanted you to go through college." I stopped after that. The sun had dropped behind the horizon and left an orange wake. The darkness was upon us. The trees turned black.

Silence came, and a wind that pushed a branch against the side of the truck didn't move either of us. John looked at the sky until it was purple, then black.

"Is that all you came to say?"

"Yes."

He drove me back to the motel.

Ela waited inside.

"I brought all your stuff from your room. You don't mind, do you?"

I shook my head.

"How'd it go?"

I shook my head.

We ate dinner, leftovers from the previous night. When we went to her room we tried to fuck, but my member wouldn't rise up to the occasion. I thought of my wife and the child we were to have.

"Sorry."

"It's all right. It's been a rough day, hasn't it?"

"It has. Johnny's probably dead," I said, though I wasn't certain if it was to legitimize my failure, or speak something I felt.

I went to sleep and woke up the next day.

Bacon sparkled in the kitchen and *Pulp Fiction* was blaring on the TV in the living room. I figured that I would call the airline today and get a flight out of here.

I had tried. Tried and failed. What was my life to amount to? Perhaps it would be in my family. And even that was a failure. What if my wife was to find out about Jenny, Ela? Couldn't I excrete some good? John wouldn't listen to me in a million years. Johnny was dead, after he had asked for help, which I had refused to give. My life's work was a few books no one read, and a job that only sowed destruction, for a nation and a company, though I had a feeling that they were one in the same.

I put on my pants, shirt, and walked into the living room. Ela's back was turned to me. I looked at the movie. A man scaring some kids. What a scene. It had seemed so alien when I saw it in high school.

My mouth salivated for the food, but I still had a horrible sense that nothing would go right in life, that this would all be for naught.

It hit me as a man started to quote the passage from the Bible. Numbers. They were numbers.

But for what?

I pulled out the papers, wrinkled to classiness. I grabbed Ela's Bible.

"Oh, good morning you."

I heard her, but it was distant, as if it wasn't spoken at all. I started to flip through the good book.

"You have a pen and paper?"

A second later she brought them to me. "What is it?"

I wrote down the numbers and looked at them. Something was familiar.

Ela shifted next to me and I remembered that she was there.

"Numbers."

"What?"

"Numbers. These passages represent numbers, that's why they don't mean anything. Or aren't coherent. He was just looking for a way to give me numbers."

She looked at the paper with passages. "It makes sense. The ampersand must be a plus. Look."

I added the numbers as prescribed in a separate column. My heart was beating fast. As if it could sniff a solution nearby.

His sentences. His sentences were off. They held something, though. They were repetitive. But what?

Nothing came. I ate breakfast, both of us standing while looking at the page.

I looked at the numbers again. Grids. In the military we had grids, but civilians had coordinates. I remembered the land navigation courses during Infantry.

"Coordinates," I said, pushing my plate aside. Ela took it and went to the kitchen.

"That's it!" she said, and moved closer to me. "Look at the first letters of his sentences."

Degrees. Minutes. Seconds. Coordinates.

"Do you have access to the Internet?"

A few hours later I was driving down to Homer Alaska as fast as I could. Ela said she would stay behind. She gave me the number of a person I could stay with, and get supplies from, in Kodiak. How do you know him? Come now, you must know I have lovers all over the world.

The numbers, everything added up to, with a quick search, a place North of the town of Kodiak. There was a ferry leaving this evening and I had to make it before then. Snow flurries slowed my progress, but I managed to make it.

Kodiak in the winter was a white icicle compared to the emerald isle I had visited in the heat of summer many years ago. I found Ela's friend, Mark. A married man with three kids. He was kind to a fault. I slept in his den and when he woke me the next day, with a large breakfast, I thanked him profusely. He never asked any questions when I asked for a shovel and GPS. Mark's beautiful wife, a gorgeous still thin five-foot brunette with green eyes eyed me with suspicion in front of him, but when he headed for work twinkled her eyes at me.

I left as soon as I could.

With the GPS, I followed a dirt road, then got off it and walked through a forest with frozen moss hanging from the trees. There was a carpet of crunchy ice and snow, and when I broke through that there was a hardened moss. The forest was enchanted. Every now and then I was certain I heard giggling of children.

I was scared.

Very scared.

But there was no time for fears. The sun would soon be gone and I had to find this spot.

I found it. Under two trees that stood together as a V.

I sat down a ways from it and just listened. When I was certain that no one was around, I walked up to the spot and dug. With a few spades of dirt and rocks I hit a box. I pulled it out. It was about as big as a carry-on suitcase. Inside was encased with several thick plastic bags. Inside that was a letter I pushed it into my pocket and stuffed the box back into its grave.

When I got back to the house I zeroed out the GPS so that nothing was saved of my trip. I thanked the man and his wife and left for the mainland on the last ferry out.

The trip back was through the edge of a storm. The captain kept reassuring us that nothing was going to happen, but the choppy waters, and the way the ferry was smacked by the waves had me leaning over the rail for the duration of the trip. The first thing I did in Anchorage was find a hostel and slept. The next day I found a library and scanned the letter onto a computer and emailed it to myself.

When I got back Ela was sitting at the office.

"You find it?"

"Another letter."

"Oh."

And I realized that I shouldn't have been that open with her.

I went into her apartment and read the letter. It was more coherent than his other ones, but it was still cryptic:

...BBB...

At last Brother;

Can you forgive me? Really find it in your heart to do so? Be the friend you always claimed you were? Be a Brother? How you must think me a madman. Relish seeing me so you can tell me off. Come on.

Come and admit it. Brother. 1 promise? Remember me. Does it sound like too much? Do the bells in your head ring? BrOther. Right now I know you are wondering why you would Ever listen to me again.

Even if you think I'm dead, I hope that you do. BrOther. Remember that time in Fairbanks? Fucked that girl after talking to her for five minutes. BrOther. I was Really happy for you then, especially since that Georgia girl had cheated on you. Georgia, never been, and never really expected to go there. Brother. 2day I'm writing this with a assault rifle in my hands. Reading victory. How many times did you talk about that book? How many times did I put up with that, huh? Brother, was that the worst thing ever. kidding, <3 ya. Respect what I'm saying right now. In these words I have said a powerful truth, BrOther. Respect. John

(my brother, remember?), he's going down a path I know that he'll be screwed, so please try to help him, for me, for old Johnny. BrOther, can you do that? Really try, though. Know that my spirit will be behind you every step of the way. Know that that spirit is grateful for having you as a friend, BrOther. Really try. Love you man. Love you, Bro. But Really try. Man, this life has been a crazy one. Matt, when you went off to war, Brother, it really freaked me out. 1 time I almost cried thinking about you dying there in some shit country for some shit reason. Really made me hate the president. Now I can breathe a sigh of relief

knowing that you are out of harms way. Now, BrOther, it feels good knowing that you'll be a normal family man. Respect, nothing but respect for all that you did. Oh, much respect. On my Brother, he'll pretend to be hard, let that slide and help him. 9times in the past few months, when these wetbacks were coming after me, tried to call him and ask for help, but couldn't do it in the end. Really a sad situation. Put all that aside and help him. Put it aside. By the way, don't think I'm crazy with this letter. I spent 8 hours trying to craft it. And if you don't know, it has a code in it. Rough stuff. Quizzed a guy I knew who went to college and he told me a few things. Quite the thing, college, shoulda gone. But there's no time for regrets, not now. 2mor is the last day for me to get out of here alive. Right, it's a hope more than anything. Really. But I've made my bed and I must sleep in it. 2mor it will be over one-way or another. Really. Seems that you were right in the end. Seems I shouldn't have tried to go up against so many people at once. Brother. 3 people know about the shit I'm in and out of all of them, you are the one I trust. Right now, it's only you. Then what is this letter trying to say? That, because I know only you will be able to crack this code, is up to you, Brother. 4 once I want you to take me seriously. Read between the lines. U can finish it out. U can do it, Brother. 6 Reasons to do this, you are a friend and I want to help you, if you crack this code, you'll find enough reward, and I hope that you will also find me. Remember me matt, remember how we talked about Victory.

later brother.

There were numbers in odd places. Like a tween's text. They didn't seem to add up to a proper coordinate. Maybe if I... No, I would not play this game.

I looked at it. An insipid anger rose within my bones and swirled up to my head. As I looked at the letter I grew furious, at myself, at Johnny, at John. At my mistakes. I was being toyed with. What could his letter possibly mean? There were no numbers, there was nothing. I wondered if I should even try. I wouldn't. Everything I had been doing recently was chasing shadows looking for answers for which I wasn't even certain of the questions. Johnny had sent me another rambling letter. Help John. Why? He was a drug dealer.

Like you Johnny, just like you.

Are you mocking me? Making me run after some foolish ghost? For all I knew Johnny was dead in some nameless grave in the valley, buried below an overpass.

Johnny, you dead fuck.

And I, a washed out veteran looking for more advice where I shouldn't. Leaving my wife in the lurch as I chose to listen to my friend who played with the law and lost, played with the black market and got fucked. Just like they said, the teachers and straight-laced people in my life. Listening to a homeless man and a stark raving-mad drug head. Are you nuts?

"What does it say?"

"It says to help his brother. To find Johnny. If he's alive."

"When was it written?"

"Doesn't say. I don't think he wants me to know that. Wanted," I corrected myself at the end. I stared at the letter for a while longer, my anger disappearing into just a sadness, like Johnny's ghost was again there. Telling me something. To hell with him.

"What are you going to do now?"

"Probably head out soon."

"What about John?"

Her face told me that she didn't like that I was giving up on this so easily. Yet, I thought, who was she to judge me for giving up on something just like that?

"I'm not certain if I can help him."

"You could try again."

I wanted to tell her off, tell her that she was a nobody old hag who should mind her own business, but I held back from doing so. Why, I wasn't certain. Johnny's ghost? Or whatever it was that I felt, the cold touch going over me and making me think about the things I had done, and how wrong I had been and how I needed to do him right.

"I could."

Her look was still admonishing me. I looked at the letter.

"Whatever you do, you do, but you came out here for a reason, didn't you? And maybe John's a hardheaded man. But what man isn't?"

"Sometimes you just have to know when to call it quits, when you're out to help a friend, or just reading the rants of a madman." I waved the paper in her face.

"Or sometimes there isn't an answer, Matt, and you have to do what's right."

"And what's that?"

"Help a friend out. You're a good man, Matt, you should know better." She walked into her bedroom.

Were we actually having a fight? I shook my head. The situations I found myself in. I looked at the number of times Johnny had written 'brother' it seemed sarcastic to me.

Or heartfelt.

And still I grasped at whatever came my way. The smart money was going home to my wife, falling into her arms, loving her, and continuing my job with Hamilton and Mr. Krysh. Get the money to raise my child and hold my nose to what I saw in my job. It would continue with or without me. But that was the weak excuse, or so the excuse we're taught about as children, that there is no excuse, especially after the Nuremberg trials, for not doing something about someone more powerful than you making you do something. Yet I was certain that there was an inherent unfairness about what I had seen, in Joes and Johnny's demises, and in all the bribes that I oversaw. And what could I do? I could make a stand.

I got into my truck and drove to John's cabins. The sun was setting again, and the darkness enveloped the forest, trucks, and cabins. There were a few lights on inside, dull, but reaching far to grab my eyes. The dogs barked and I saw a man come out on the porch with a shotgun. I hadn't seen him before. About six-feet tall, he had a handlebar moustache and a large belly underneath a flannel shirt and ripped jeans. He didn't look pleased.

I pulled my truck so my window was next to him and rolled it down.

"Who the fuck are you?"

"I'm Matt. Is John here?"

He eyed me for a few seconds before calling John. John stepped up to my car as the other person walked back inside.

"What is it?"

"I just wanted to say that... that if you need any help, I can help you."

"What ya mean?"

"I mean, I know things. I can help. Help you fight, help you avoid surveillance. I can help. Stay off cell phones..."

"Stay off cell phones? Like I wouldn't know that? Look, I don't need your help. Got it? I don't need some old veteran coming here thinking he can do some good."

He held my stare. I thought he might have been tearing up, but it could have just been the cold dry air.

John turned and walked back into the cabin.

I left the next day, Ela came to see me off at the airport, friendly, not looking too bad, though at that moment I wanted to put as much distance between us as possible. Not to say that I hated her. There was more of a connection between us than I would have thought; I would even venture to use the word love. Before I left, and after an odd silence she said: you should trust your instincts more.

I slept on the entire plane trip back, Johnny's letter in my pocket. There was nothing to do. I wasn't going to waste my life on some code that made no sense. But I promised myself that everyday I would glance at it. See if something came to me, that way no one could say that I gave up on my friend.

At the 205th station Smellgood was gone. Probably moved to another station to collect change. Another bum walked up and down the platform, dressed in jeans and a jean jacket, white beard, skin as black as coal, and he muttered to himself, incoherent ramblings about the Bronx. The whole station smelled like smoke and urine. It seemed fitting.

My wife hugged me at home and I felt glad to be with her. No one else mattered as much as her, I reminded myself. But there was still good to be done.

"I should tell you something, honey." I led her to our bed and we lied down next to each other. "If I've been distant recently, it's because of a few things."

"Johnny?"

"Johnny is partially it."

"Did you find him?"

"No, I found his brother, who wanted nothing to do with me."

"Well, you have to let somethings be sometimes."

I held my breath. I wanted to talk, to let out all the air inside me. "I suppose." And I knew then that I didn't want any advice from anyone, that maybe I had never been seeking advice. For some reason, I had been hoping that this confession would tie a loose knot between us, but it felt like my old lady was now drifting away, far away, that instead of being on the bed next to me, her heart beating with mine, she was across the city on the phone, just about to go through a tunnel. I was going to tell her about Joe, maybe Jenny, but decided that those things would only increase the distance. We ordered food that night and I got a call from Hamilton about some work the next day.

In the village the next day, getting used to all the bustle, after the quiet of the Alaskan forests, I saw Jenny. Or rather, she saw me, tapped my shoulder.

"Hi stranger. What have you been up to?"

"Busy," I said, with a hint of desire that she seemed to pick up on. She was gorgeous: her tights were held nicely by her thighs and short gray skirt, and her striped shirt highlighted her breasts and dwindling waist. Be true, be good.

"Well, too busy to even call?"

There was a hint of hurt, and I believed it. "Sorry."

"Do you want to come up for old times sake?"

Her and Hamilton. What was that about?

"Sure thing."

Her apartment was like an old friend, nothing had really changed about it. She stepped up to me and kissed me as she kicked the door shut with her heel.

"God, I missed you." Her hand ran over my crotch. "Your cock."

My heart was racing, my mind was pushing me into her, my body melded close to her warmth, her beauty. No, be good, as questions. Leave.

"Jenny," I pulled away from her. The image of my wife with my child inside her. The image of Jenny and Hamilton. These could not not matter. "What is it you do?"

Her look told two tales: one was she knew exactly what I was getting at; the other that she was innocent of all charges. She was good. I should have known better than to get involved with her. Any algorithm behavior she had presented initially was only to capture me. Her and Hamilton, I reminded myself.

"What do you mean?"

She wasn't going to play. And of course, I would have been a fool to expect anything from her.

"I have to go."

"Why?" She *did* seem genuinely hurt. Perhaps her motives were not all sinister. But how could I ever know?

"Sorry, I can't do this to my wife."

I opened the door and started down the stairs.

I felt her eyes on my back, her hand's ghost still on my cock, as I walked down and out of her building.

I met Hamilton in a different building near Columbus Circle. He had an office on the 20th floor. His face seemed ever the mask.

"We have to get going back to Dubai in a few days. You can make it?"

"Of course."

"I want to make sure that there are no misunderstandings. Got it?"

"Got it," I said, though I wasn't certain what he was talking about. Was he talking about the previous statements he had made to me? I was here, wasn't I? But I had to do some good. Whatever it was this company did, it was not right.

His secretary, a perky twenty-something year-old in a tight dress-suit, poked her head in. "Your two o'clock is here Mr. Hamilton."

He ruffled some papers, said, "see you soon," and ran out.

I stuck my hands in my pocket. The view from his window was of the bustling traffic circle, a monument in the middle that seemed to mean nothing. On Hamilton's desk was a flash drive. It was the one he kept around his neck. This would be the start. I looked around the office. There were no cameras here. Of course there weren't. I stepped up to the flash drive and picked it up. The secrets it must have held.

"Oh there it is." Hamilton was behind me, his hand out.

"I... I was going to return it,"

"Of course you were." He smiled at me, but his eyes were knives.

I felt a coldness rise up from my feet. Then anger at myself for being scared. I had faced off with bombs, and murderers, and been in ambushes and firefights, but something about this place, Hamilton's look, made me shiver.

"Can you wait here for me?"

"Sure."

I stood there and watched car after car go past the monument. A few people walked by it, but no one stopped to look at it. An ode to good luck. I thought of some of the passages that Johnny had written. He had spoken some truth when he sent me that letter.

"Matt, have a seat." Hamilton walked in and locked the door behind him.

I sat down, no longer felt scared, but calm.

"Matt." Hamilton turned his computer monitor so that I could see it. "You *do* remember what I asked a while ago?"

"About what?"

He let out some air in a hiss sound, as if he was losing his patience. "Do you know your place?"

I stayed quiet.

"You left your laptop open today."

"I don't know..."

"I wasn't asking. You left it open. Look."

I looked to see what would be the view of my apartment from my desk where I kept my laptop. It was my webcam, I felt weak, like I had to take a piss.

"Yes, keep looking."

My wife came into the view, then disappeared again. My weakness turned to a furious anger. There was no one else in this room, I could leap across the table and kill Hamilton. Rip his throat out. That was my wife he was messing with.

"I know, from your background, that you want to kill me. You probably could do it in a second if you wanted, but give me a moment," he texted something on his phone, then turned up the volume on his computer.

"The thing is, after watching you, your wife really loves you. Fully. Doesn't know anything about your..."

I was hit by a sense of evil sadness. How it felt, I couldn't quite describe. I think then I knew what Johnny had felt, why I was so angry at him, so pissed because he was so much like me, and when he needed it I didn't help, not because of anything other than when I was in his situation no one was going to help me. I felt sorry for his brother for being so angry, but I had a sense of why he refused to take my offer for help.

Hamilton stayed quiet, observed me like some animal in the wild.

I felt sorry, most of all, for my wife, for having been *this* to her. I felt the sadness, it could have been Johnny's ghost, or Joe's ghost, or it could have been future ghosts, or merely the sense that my powers, the great things I thought I had done or could do, in this world had been shadows.

"Are we clear?"

I looked at my feet and nodded my head. It had never been clear—the everything else—to me, it never had been and never would be, it just wasn't for me to know, but was what clear was that which was required of me.

"Two days."

"Two days," I repeated, like I was scared of someone slapping me across the face. I got up and had to hold the chair to stop from falling over.

The End

About the Author:

Nelson Lowhim was born in Tanzania where he lived for the first decade of his life. He then lived in India for a year before finally settling in the U.S. in the state of Michigan. He spent some of his formative years hitchhiking and hiking around the great state of Alaska. From there he joined the Army and served for seven years as an Infantryman in 1st AD then as an Engineer in Fifth Group. After his time in the Military—which included many travels through Europe and the Middle East—he came to New York and earned an undergraduate degree from Columbia University. He currently lives with his girlfriend in the Bronx.

Connect with me online (and tell me what you think):

Smashwords: http://www.smashwords.com/profile/view/nlowhim

My blog: http://nelsonlowhim.blogspot.com/

Facebook: http://www.facebook.com/nlowhim